She put her head on my shoulder. Her hand slid off my thigh and into my lap, paused. She kissed my ear, lingered there. "And what are you afraid of?" she whispered.

"Afraid you'll stop," I said against the moist spread of her lips.

"I couldn't," she answered, falling back on the divan, taking me with her. "Not for a long, long time," she said beside me. She took my hand and guided it beneath her sweater to the warmth of bare breast. "Feel my heart," she said. "I'm a fast train on a down track to nowhere. And my heart says; *Couldn't stop— wouldn't stop—couldn't if I would—wouldn't if I could...*"

The Star Trap

Robert Colby

PROLOGUE BOOKS

F+W Media, Inc.

Published in electronic format by
PROLOGUE BOOKS
an imprint of F+W Media, Inc.
10151 Carver Road
Blue Ash, Ohio 45242
www.prologuebooks.com

eISBN 10: 1-4405-3686-4
eISBN 13: 978-1-4405-3686-1
POD ISBN 10: 1-4405-5515-X
POD ISBN 13: 978-1-4405-5515-2

This is a work of fiction. Names, characters, corporations, institutions,
organizations, events, or locales in this novel are either the product of the author's
imagination or, if real, used fictitiously. The resemblance of any character to actual
persons (living or dead) is entirely coincidental.

This work has been previously published as a Gold Medal Book by:
Fawcett Publications, Inc., Greenwich, Conn.

1...

The phone was ringing by my bed. The sound came to me through the fuzz of sleep and too much alcohol. Hours earlier—how many I didn't know—I had been in high flight from the inescapable truth: my small world was foundering badly.

The bell tinkled distantly, opening a tiny wedge in my consciousness. And then closed in, strong, shrill, demanding.

I groped for the lamp on the night table, found the switch, squinted at my watch. It was twenty-five minutes to three A.M. I fumbled for the phone.

"My God," I said into the mouthpiece, "whoever you are, go 'way. You've just made an enemy."

"Glenn! Is that you, Glenn?"

The voice was female. It had the breathless quality of controlled hysteria.

"Who is it?" I said.

"Is this Glenn Harley?"

"Yes, yes. What do you want and who the hell—"

"This is Nancy Rhymer. Glenn, I—I need your help."

I swung my legs out of bed and sat up, wide awake. Nancy Rhymer! I had never heard her voice on the phone. And yet the sound of it, when connected with her name, was electric. She was of another world, the fringe

5

of which I had barely touched, but the image of her, captured in those rare meetings, was etched in the secret recesses of my mind—where I kept unattainable treasures for inspection.

"Is it really Nancy Rhymer?" I said. "This is no time for a gag, three o'clock in the morning."

"Four months ago, at the Key Club," she said quickly. "Remember?"

I remembered. "It's a pleasant shock, Nancy. What can I do for you?"

"Glenn, dear, I'm in trouble."

She had never called me dear or anything like it. "What kind of trouble, Nancy?"

"A very special kind that you can't talk about on the phone. Can you come to my place?"

Her voice sounded like thin glass cracking.

"Why do you need me, Nancy? You have so many friends."

"Glenn, Glenn!" she cried. "I'm in a jam. Will you come? Will you?"

"I'll come, Nancy."

"You remember the way?"

"I remember. In about . . . twenty minutes."

"Make it fifteen. Or . . . or I'll just fall apart. Do hurry!"

"Try to be calm, Nancy. I'm on the way."

I hung up.

And scrambled into my clothes.

6

2...

My apartment was in a building on Franklin, just off Sunset Boulevard in Hollywood. I raced downstairs into my aging Chevy and gunned over to the Strip. Traffic was light at that hour, the November air was cool and damp, and there was a suggestion of fog in the misty hue of street lamps. Watching for squad cars, I rammed ahead toward Beverly Hills.

Nancy Rhymer had a small house high up, on the very rim of Coldwater Canyon. From the picture window in her living room you looked straight down into the Canyon, a magic arena emblazoned with a million lights. There was a feeling that you hung suspended in the clouds. The view was fantastically beautiful.

I had been there only once before, at a party. Nancy was surrounded by the great and near-great of the movie industry. She invited me on a whim, that night about four months ago when I ran into her at the Key Club. And then she all but ignored me. As did everyone else. I was miserably lonely at the party, especially since I had come down with an incurable love sickness after my first exposure to Nancy. I had hoped that the party would give me at least a few minutes in some separate corner with her—long enough to make her more definitely aware of me. But she was always on stage, playing her scene to

7

the VIP's in the first row. I was just another anonymous face in the gallery.

At the height of the revelry I crept away without saying good-bye. And didn't hear from Nancy again. Until now.

Nancy never got to be a star. She was a starlet, one of those bright shadows that dances onto the screen for a few empty lines, then dances off again into the oblivion between pictures. She was not terribly photogenic and her acting ability didn't seem special—though who can tell in a few feet of film? But in person, from my view at least, she was more sweetly put together, more exciting, than any of her big-box-office sisters.

I first met her two years before when we both had walk-on bits in a television drama. She came from a small town near Denver, the name of which I've forgotten. There she had been big in Little Theatre, and had wanted to be big in Hollywood. The same old story. There are hundreds like her. Except that, even at twenty-two, she had a certain maturity. She didn't just gaze off into the pink heavens of her future. She came knowing it was tough. She got a part-time job modeling in a dress shop over on Wilshire.

Ours was an odd, one-sided relationship. She was friendly, she talked shop with me, made dry, cynical comments on The Game. But I never could get very close to her at those unexpected times we met. She seemed not so much uninterested in me, as closed away in the vehicle she was riding so desperately toward the top. She had no time for minor-league players. If she was one herself, she thought of it as only temporary and circumstantial. When I asked her for a date she never said no, just "Call me." But when I did, someone always said she was out.

I kept wondering what would happen if she ever took one long look. And saw what was concealed in my eyes.

We were both members of the Key Club. Just a bar,

8

really, with booths and a few tables. Your own key was admission to the front door. Dozens of places like it around the country. But here the trade was radio and TV, a few lesser movie people.

Sometimes I would find her alone at the bar, nursing a drink, looking thoughtful and a little sad. Men shouldered each other to get near her, but she preferred to be alone and could turn on a look that was like a yawn in the face. That did it most of the time. I knew she was not bored but self-protective. I made my conversation impersonal, and for this she tolerated me.

Sometimes she would get up and put a coin in the juke machine, and then I would be able to stare at her frankly. She was a little less than tall but carried herself as if reaching gracefully for stature. Her hair was long and brown with glistening overtones of red. Her face was heart-shaped, intense and utterly delicate. Her eyes were wide, deep brown and calmly, innocently provocative. Her mouth was a masterpiece of soft demand.

She was so slim, so narrow of waist and hip that her body was a showcase for the high mold of her breasts.

She seemed built for all things tender and sensual, while her eyes and manner intriguingly denied the knowledge of sex.

During the first two years that I knew Nancy, I had some small success as a TV actor. Perhaps more because I was a persistent knocker on doors than because of any great talent. I used to call at the ad agencies so frequently that sometimes I would walk in at the very moment when a director was looking through the files for a husky young actor like me with decent enough features to play second-string lover. Or tough guy. Or any character. I used to hang around the halls of CBS and NBC, outside the studios where the shows were in rehearsal. And corner the Wheel in charge when he came out.

I got parts. But I always felt they were handouts.

In that time, Nancy and I ran almost apace. She was a little behind, a little more hungry. She lived in a cheap boarding house, scrounged for meals and clothes. Then suddenly, overnight, she was in that house on the rim of the Canyon. A starlet. With a contract. And she seemed to have more possessions and money than she earned. More important people than you would expect came to her little parties. I seldom saw her at all.

But I used to wonder about her, and keep my ears open. Because no one suspected my real interest, I heard things. At first that she was a rare species in Hollywood, a gal who played it the hard way. No parking in cars. No sleeping around. She warmed no beds for her parts.

Some said she was a sweet little virgin. Some said she was frigid. Some even made bets about her. But no one could be found who really knew. And in the eyes of the cynical, everyone-has-their-price wolves, she was an irritation. They seemed to have a compulsive need to undo her. To soil her as so many of the others were soiled.

Then, when she became a starlet, when she moved up the Canyon and I lost sight of her, I began to hear other things. That she was traveling with a fast crowd in the power clique. That she had changed. That some of her parties were openly wild. And others were secret and sordid. There were hints of orgies—with a wink and a sly smile to underline all that the name implied.

I believed none of this. Labeled it as the bitter gossip of the jealous. The party I had attended was wild enough—but not in any orgiastic sense. Not while I was there. And anyway, I wanted to believe in the picture of Nancy still uncompromised. More than that, I had seen something in her eyes. A determination to be above the shallow evil of bed-to-bed success. The undercurrents of her needing would take her to bed. But with the one guy she loved.

I tried to forget about her, tried to keep her from

10

becoming a kind of morbid obsession that would upset the balance of my life. I told myself that I should know better, that I was a big boy now, not a mooning adolescent. It was unhealthy to torment myself with this silly goddam love dream of Nancy Rhymer and Glenn Harley riding off into the sunset on an eternal honeymoon.

I made myself busy with my work. I chased around with an assortment of well-stacked dames, one or two of them just as beautifully assembled as Nancy—and twice as willing. A week or two would go by when I didn't give Nancy a thought. And then some idiot would drop her name casually into the garbage pail of small talk, or I would see some girl on the street who from a distance was her poor replica. In an instant I would fall silent and moody, that old scratchy record of abysmal longing for Nancy spinning crazily in my head.

Meanwhile, some of the shows in which I was occasionally performing changed sponsors. And producers. The ones who were hiring me. Other shows collapsed—were hurried into early graves by poor ratings from the little men who compile the big figures on public boredom. And at thirty-four, when I should have been climbing to some lofty niche, I was sliding dangerously. I was barely existing.

And then I got the call. Twenty-five minutes to three A.M. From Nancy Rhymer.

Just in front of the Beverly Hills Hotel on Sunset, I spun right a ways, then left. After a mile or so I drove onto a narrow road and spiraled upward sharply. Occasionally my headlights caught a few dark-faced inset houses, clusters of trees, dirt-walled cliffs. Tires shrieked around tight S-curves shrouded in patches of fog. Once I skidded and almost lost control at a place near the top where the road bent left, and straight ahead was only space.

And all the time I couldn't think of a single reason why Nancy Rhymer would need my help at three o'clock

11

in the morning. Nancy, who had dozens of important friends and, if necessary, the whole police department at the other end of her phone.

At last the road pushed over the top and I followed it around the edge of the Canyon to Nancy's house. A coral-pink stucco. No lights showed. A pale-blue sedan, a Lincoln Continental, squatted in front.

But Nancy had a Buick convertible, yellow. When I got out I was just able to see the shine of the rear deck protruding from her carport. I had no idea who owned the Lincoln. It made me uneasy. Had she called someone else?

There was a fence with a gate. The gate stood ajar. I closed it silently behind me and went up the walk. I knocked. The door opened immediately. There was the flutter of a silken garment, then a hand grabbed my wrist and pulled me inside. The door closed.

"Wait there, Glenn." Nancy's voice was a hoarse whisper.

A light came on across the room. A dim blue light from a table lamp. It gave an eerie visibility.

"My stargazing light," said Nancy in a husky, nervous way. She stood in the blue glow, staring toward me. She wore a thin negligee open at the top enough so that I could see a nightgown beneath. The right shoulder strap had been torn and dangled down in front. The long swell of one naked breast was revealed almost to the nipple.

I saw that Nancy had a glass in her hand. Now she gulped from it, peered at me and still said nothing.

"Are you alone, Nancy?"

"You might say that," she answered. "I don't know." She giggled. It was an unpleasant sound. It stopped abruptly.

"Are you boozed up, Nancy? Is that all it is?"

She shook her head.

"Then get hold of yourself, honey. Tell me what's wrong."

12

She fluttered around the room, checked drapes on the street side. They were pulled tight. She drained the glass, set it down and moved toward me, swaying slightly. She grazed my cheek with the fingers of one soft hand. Never before had she touched me. Or stood so sweetly-smelling, overpoweringly near.

"I need your help," she said. "I need you, Glenn."

"I know. That's why I'm here, for God's sake. What is it? What is it!"

"I'll show you."

She took my hand and led me toward that picture window. I looked down. Far below there was now only a pale smattering of lights; great areas were in darkness.

"Did you think I brought you here for the view?" Her voice so close by my ear startled me. "You're looking in the wrong direction."

Her head swung right, slowly, and down.

The body of a man lay before a sofa, almost at my feet. He was flat on his back, one leg drawn partly up.

I sucked in a giant breath, stood gazing for a long time at the crimson spread on his white shirt before I moved to bend over him.

13

3...

I could barely see in that blue-lighted gloom. There was a lamp standing near the sofa and in a daze I felt around for the switch. Behind me Nancy sobbed, "No, Glenn, no!" I turned on the light.

You read about all forms of violent death in the newspapers. Including murder. And with the words there are sometimes pictures. But the words are meaningless details about dream people in a dream world apart from yours, and the still forms in the pictures are just broken dolls. But to stare for the first time at the reality of violent death just by your feet is an awesome experience.

He was six feet of lean but muscular man in slacks the color of okra, a tan cashmere sport coat, and a white shirt open at the throat. From mid-chest down, the shirt was drenched in blood already dry enough to have lost the first brilliance of color. More blood pooled around him on the parquet floor.

He was young. Touching thirty, perhaps. You could tell that he didn't like to cut that black wavy hair. It hadn't known shears in weeks. He had heavy brows and jaw, a puffy sensual mouth. He might once have been handsome in the manner of the sneeringly suave. The skin was naturally dark and had been enriched by long

14

baking in the sun. But now this darkness was fading, was toned with a sickly gray which seemed to rise from beneath the surface of the skin.

The eyes were rolled back, the mouth open, the expression one of faint surprise, as if death had come at the instant when the mind was posing some momentous question.

I felt a stirring in my stomach, a lightness in the head, like the time the dentist pulled a wisdom tooth and held the gory thing up for my inspection. I covered my eyes, leaned against the couch, couldn't think.

There was only the rasp of Nancy's frightened breathing.

After a moment I knelt down and forced my eyes to fasten again on the man's face. I had a strange reaction. I didn't know him at all, but he was remarkably familiar.

Slowly, I opened his shirt. The wound was hard to find in that dark matting of blood-caked hair on his chest. A narrow, vertical incision that seemed, on the surface, too small to kill a man. Small, but probably deep. Not a bullet wound. A knife cut.

I turned to look up at Nancy. "You did this?"

Her negligee was still open and she seemed unaware of the exposure of one thrusting pink-white breast, which perversely demanded a small corner of my attention. She looked like a little girl who wanted desperately to laugh in church. Or at a funeral. But as I watched, her teeth clamped so tightly over the soft petal of her lower lip that a small drop of blood coursed down her chin.

"You did this?" I said again.

Almost imperceptibly, she nodded.

"I've seen him before. Who is he?"

She brushed at a lock of hair, her mouth trembling.

"Norm, Norman Rainey," she said in a small voice. And began to sag.

I jumped up and caught her in my arms, too aware of her body against me, ashamed of my instant reaction.

15

"Norman Rainey," I said. "Of course! Used to play the heavy. Starred in a couple of adventure films last year. B-grade stuff."

Her head was on my shoulder. "He's the one," she breathed against my neck.

She began to cry. Between sobs she said, "Please, oh please, turn off the light." I did. But I left that ghastly blue one lighted against total darkness. Then I settled her on a daybed across the room and let her cry it out.

Meanwhile I paced, found a liquor cabinet and a rack of glasses. I poured myself a stiff one. When Nancy had quieted, I brought her one, too, and as she sipped, I drew up a chair and waited. She became conscious that I was watching her. For the first time she looked down at her breasts. Slowly she closed the negligee around her. Then we sat staring at each other.

"Tell me," I said.

She gulped the rest of her drink, set the glass on a coffee table, drew fingers under her eyes.

"There isn't time now for all of it," she said in a voice of forced control. "I don't even know where to begin. . . . I've tried to keep myself decent in this—this ratrace of grimy hands always reaching for you, trying to pull you down into a bed still warm from the last affair. But I seemed to attract the very thing I didn't want."

I could understand why. Nancy was not merely a sexy woman. She was the unusual one, out of the millions of drab creatures, who seemed designed by nature for the single, urgent purpose of love-making. Her denial was a challenge.

"Go on," I said. Coldly. Because I was full of mixed emotions.

"Please!" she said. "Please don't sit there as if we had hours to fool away. Every minute that passes . . ."

"You called me in the middle of the night," I said. "Suddenly, after all this time, you need me. You want my

16

help. Not simply help. Just to tell you what to do about a dead man, a murder that will be screaming headlines in every newspaper in the country. For that maybe I should have an explanation, Nancy. Before I advise you to call the police and then beat it out of here and hope to God no one will ever know I came."

They were only words. Looking at Nancy, I knew as I said them that I would help her to the farthest extreme, if her reason to kill left me the slightest room for self-respect. Yet, for all the hovering I had done outside the closed door of her, I wanted her to know I wasn't easy.

"I promise," she pleaded, "that later—later I'll tell you every godawful detail that led up to this thing. But for now, it's not important for you to know anything but that Norman Rainey was the worst kind of cruel, sneaky animal. That he tricked me into his own personal gutter. At a time when I was clean. When no man had touched me. And then he came here tonight drunk. And tried to rape me."

"The bastard," I said. "And you simply defended yourself?"

"Yes."

"Self-defense. Justifiable. So why don't you call the police?"

"Glenn, Glenn!" she cried. "You just said yourself that every paper in the country would grab it. Weeks of notoriety. Insinuations. Pictures. Reporters hounding me. An ugly trial."

"Your career is important to you, isn't it, Nancy?"

"Beyond saying."

"It's a lousy thought," I said. "But he's dead and it wasn't your fault. It's negative publicity. But there would be sympathy for you. The picture people would capitalize on those headlines. They'd make you a star, Nancy. Overnight."

"Yes," she said. "So that grubby little people could look at me on the screen and think lewd thoughts about

17

me. No, I want to rise on talent, not smut. Besides, if I had to go through with this, I couldn't stand the ordeal. I can hide behind a fictional character, but I cringe against that kind of public nakedness. It would kill me."

She got a cigarette from a tray in front of her and stuck it in her mouth, where it trembled between her lips. I made the light, watched her exhale on a long sigh.

"Nancy, I don't see a better way out for you than to tell the truth."

"But I can't! There are things which would come out. In which I was forced to become involved. Sordid. Evil. I could never face those things and live. Everything would be gone. Ask me to kill myself, and I would sooner do that."

I believed her.

"What are these things which would come out, Nancy?"

She was silent.

"All right," I said. "So you got yourself into a mess. You've got a whole heap of dirty laundry in the closet. And you'd rather die than hang it out in public view for the scandal sheets. All right. I believe you. Maybe you got sucked in by your own crazy ambition. You wouldn't be the first one. Whatever you've done, I'm not going to condemn you. But this is not just some embarrassing little midnight brawl you want straightened out. That guy over there is not only famous, he's very dead. I could go to jail just for being in the same room with his body without calling the police. Now—don't you think I ought to know all about it before I decide to jump in with both feet?"

"Yes, yes, yes! But listen," she pleaded. "It's a very long story, terribly complex. And right now I couldn't even make sense out of it for you. I haven't time. Later, of course. Later. All right? Because every minute, every second we delay—"

18

"What was it, Nancy, some kind of a sex thing? Is that why you don't want to talk about it?"

"Yes. I mean, no, that isn't why I . . . It's a matter of time, time, time!" she cried. "Won't you understand that?"

"You killed Rainey out of revenge, is that it? You got him over here and then you—"

"No!"

"Or was it jealousy? You killed him in a wild fit of jealousy."

"Oh, no, no! I didn't mean to kill him. I was frightened. He was attacking me."

"Okay. We'll skip the sordid involvement bit. For the time being. But I want to know exactly what happened. Never mind the past. Just what happened here tonight. And all of it."

"All right," she said meekly. "And then you'll help me?"

"You don't know what you're asking."

"Yes, I do."

"I'll try to think of something. Just tell me the truth."

She got up, walked in that blue fog of light to the liquor cabinet, poured herself half a glassful, turned.

"I seldom drink, you know. It does frightening things to me. But now . . ." She swallowed, moved toward me, stopped, hung her head and spoke to her feet.

"I knew Norman Rainey in a number of ways. Too well. He was starring in a Western, one of those epic things. It's on location now in Nevada. For his part, he was finished with it. But then they called him for some retakes. He was driving there tonight. He had had more than enough to drink and, on an impulse, I guess, he stopped by here to try and persuade me to go with him.

"It was about two o'clock this morning. I haven't been sleeping well, and I was reading in bed. The bell rang and I went to answer. It was Norman. He just pushed his

19

way in without a word, and once I had the door open I couldn't stop him. He spent about a minute leering at me, made some suggestive remarks, then insisted that I ride along with him to location. He was going to drive the rest of the night, and he was lonely. If we got really, really tired we could stop at a cozy motel, he said.

"I said some very emphatic things to him and told him to get out. He grabbed me. He reminded me that we were very much alone and I shouldn't resist. The things he said and the things he did are too obscene for repeating. But when he began to haul me into the bedroom I broke away. He was right behind me.

"I dashed for the kitchen, opened a drawer and got out a carving knife. I backed away into the living room. He followed. Over there." She pointed to where Rainey lay. " 'Nancy,' he said, 'I'm going to take that away from you. And then you're going to be one sorry bitch.' "

Nancy took another drink and a new expression came to her face. A kind of self-hypnosis, a fascination that was almost pleasure.

"I lowered the knife. But when he was almost on top of me, I lifted it high." She made a great upheaving motion with her arm. "And then . . . and then I brought it down!" Her balled fist dropped like a guillotine and her face was savage. "He gave a little gasp. And he clutched at me. But his hands came loose. I never let go of the knife, and he just fell away from me and collapsed on the floor."

As if the effort had exhausted her, Nancy's shoulders drooped and she sank into a chair.

It was as though I had seen the struggle. For half a minute I wasn't able to speak. Then I crossed to her and leaned over her chair. I lifted her chin, and made her look at me.

"Nancy, at a time like this, why would you call *me*?"

"Because I couldn't think of another soul who wouldn't betray me sooner or later."

20

I looked into her eyes. "You guessed, didn't you?"

"I didn't guess. I knew. Even before you did."

I got down on my knees and put my arms around her. She pulled my head to her breast.

"Nancy, Nancy, what is it you want me to do?"

She took a great breath. "Get rid of him. Make him gone. So they'll never know. So I'll never have to think about him again."

My lips were against her flesh. I had had two years of longing. Desire in perfumed waves broke over me. I pulled away to look at her.

"Do you realize," I said, "that if I'm able to do this for you, I'll be part of it?"

"Yes."

"And if I'm part of it, I can't help but be part of you. If power over you is what I want, you give me full power. It's like an unbreakable contract."

"Yes, yes. I know."

And then, for the first time in my life, I kissed her.

4...

"It's almost four o'clock," I said. "We'll have to hurry." Again I was pacing while Nancy sat tensely forward in her chair. "We'll have to get rid of his car. And he should disappear altogether. Just vanish. It may be years before they stop looking for him, but eventually the fuss will die down. Now the first, last and most important question is, did anyone know he was coming here?"

"No."

"How can you be sure?"

Nancy smoked furiously. There was hope and even excitement in her face.

"Well," she said, "before it got out of hand we talked for a few minutes. He said that earlier he had been over at Marvin Grinstead's house and—"

"Grinstead? The producer?"

"Yes."

"He's an independent. Right?"

"Right. He's doing this Western."

"I've heard tales about him. That he has gambling interests in Vegas and that this movie business is a sideline, a hobby."

"Not a hobby. An obsession. He's got practically everything he owns tied up in that Western. In fact, he's always broke and scheming up filthy and illegal ways to get money."

"What kind of illegal ways to get money?" I asked.

She looked up at me with a pained expression, her face pale and drawn.

"You promised," she said.

"I promised what?"

"Not to probe. Not now."

"Just give me a hint, then. What kind of a racket is Grinstead operating?"

"Oh my God, Glenn! Help me! We have things to do!"

"*I* have things to do, you mean. Without me nothing will be done, and you know it, Nancy. C'mon, c'mon. For all I know, Grinstead killed Rainey and left you to cover for him."

"Me! Why should I cover *anything* for Marvin Grinstead? I detest him."

"Why? Because you're caught in his racket and you do as you're told. That's a pretty good guess, isn't it?"

"No!" She caught my hand, her face pleading. "I've told you the truth about what happened, Glenn. All of it. I mean, about tonight."

"All right. And in the background somewhere is Grinstead. Where does he fit? What's this filthy racket of his you speak of?"

"He squeezes people. Little people and big people. He's like an evil god. He tempts with sin and then holds the sinners in a prison of fear until they pay. The little people pay with service—in slavery. The big people pay with money."

"Double-talk. Just double-talk, Nancy."

"There are things I don't understand," she said. "But Marvin is the organizer and the front. It begins with him and he has a whole network of dirty little men working for him. They stop at nothing. I'm frightened, Glenn. I could die for telling what I know."

23

"And you could die in the gas chamber for what happened tonight."

"That's it," she moaned. "That's why we've got to hurry."

"You haven't told me one damn thing, Nancy. But you're right. There isn't time now, and I'm going to take your word for it that soon you'll explain what this mess tonight has to do with Grinstead and some super con game. Now, what about Norman Rainey? We've got to follow his movements to see if there's a chance anyone knew he was coming here. You said that earlier he was at Grinstead's house. Right?"

"Yes. Grinstead had been in conference with Norman, wanted him to get off to Nevada in the morning to do retakes on location there. Norman didn't tell Grinstead he was coming here because he didn't know it himself. He had been drinking and when he got home he didn't want to go to bed. So, on a whim, he packed and came over here with his little plan. I was to drive with him as far as Vegas and fly back.

"He would never have come here unless he was drunk, because he knew I hated him. But it wasn't until he got home that he decided. So, you see, Grinstead knew nothing about it."

"Good. Was Rainey married?"

"Divorced."

"So he lived alone?"

"Yes."

"Did he come here directly from his house?"

"Well, I didn't question him much, naturally. But he definitely implied that. In any case, he's . . . he was close-mouthed about what he did. Because he did a lot of very nasty things."

"All right," I said. "But we'll take out some insurance. If ever someone claims Rainey mentioned he was on his way here, you say he phoned first. You had been asleep and were angry. You told him he definitely couldn't come over. Got that?"

24

"Sounds logical."

Looking across the room, I had the shuddering realization that we were actually talking about a dead man who lay in his own blood a few feet away. I kicked the thought from my mind. It was a mighty effort.

"My God, my God, Glenn," she said suddenly. "What will we do with him? A lake somewhere? The woods?"

"No," I said. "Too risky. I'm always reading in the papers how some body is discovered in a remote place by the merest chance. Kids, hunters, fishermen, bums on the prowl. . . . The body should be where we can keep an eye on it, so to speak."

"Oh, Glenn!"

"I know. But now we have to talk and think in terms of something inanimate which must be hidden in the best possible way. It should be in a place where people have no right to trespass, to snoop around."

"Glenn! What are you saying?"

"Just about what you think. That he should be buried on the grounds here."

"No!"

I went over and took her by the shoulders. "Listen, Nancy. Listen to me. Every mistake, every forbidden act has its penalty. This is yours. You'll have to live with it. Or change your mind about going to the police."

"No. I can't ever do that." She began to pace, wringing her hands. "I can't change my mind. I can't tell the truth. I want to. Believe me, Glenn, I want to. I'd like to let the whole rotten business come out, let all the slimy people connected with it go down the drain. But then I'd be a public spectacle—something degraded and grotesque. It wouldn't matter that I fell into a pit while running toward fame and success. There'd be no place to hide, not even from myself. And one night I'd reach for those pills in the medicine cabinet. And I'd take them all. Every one."

"Well then, Nancy?"

25

She stood still for a long moment, staring at me.

"Where?" she said. "Where would we. . . . Where would we . . ."

"Bury him?"

"Yes." She began to cry softly. "Yes, where?"

"You know the property better than I do. Snap out of it, Nancy, and think. Think!"

She wiped her eyes, straightened. A look of determination tightened her face.

"There's yard on either side of the house, screened by that fence."

"How close is the nearest neighbor?"

"Quite a ways. I picked this place for privacy. And even if there weren't a fence, it's dark."

"The sides of the house seem vulnerable," I said. "Naturally, the front is out."

"And the back," she said, "is the view side. It drops straight down. . . . Or does it? Wait a minute!"

She got up and went to the window. I followed.

"Look below there," she said. "Can you see that tree?"

I looked and I saw dimly in the moonlight, fifty feet or so down, a small dirt-and-rock ledge with a single tree.

"That's it!" I said. "Pray for soft ground. I don't suppose you have anything like a rope."

"I have lots of new clothesline. Two coils of it."

"A shovel?"

"My God, no!"

"That's great! And we can't do without it. There's one around my apartment house. Oh, goddam, if I had only known . . ."

We nearly laughed. But not quite.

"Get dressed," I said. "We have to get rid of his car, anyway. I'll drive it, you take yours, and we'll leave mine here. He won't be missed for a day or two. By that time I'll have his car repainted and in storage, with another set of license tags. Meanwhile we'll park it in a garage and then pick up the shovel."

26

She scampered into the bedroom and was dressed in two minutes. While she was gone, I had the nauseating job of finding the car keys in his pocket.

Outside, I opened the trunk of the Lincoln. I found a suitcase and brought it into the house. On the way down the long, winding hill, with Nancy following in her car, I looked in the glove compartment. I was amazed to find a fully loaded .38 revolver. I dropped it in my pocket.

At four-thirty A.M. we had parked the Lincoln in an all-night garage and picked up the shovel. We sped back in the blackest of darkness under what had now become a clouding, starless sky.

5...

"Now, Nancy," I said, "you'll have to take his feet. I'll support the bulk of him."

She squeezed her eyes shut once before she bent down, but her face was expressionless as stone. I had an old raincoat which I always kept in the car, and we had it fastened around him to keep any blood from trailing. We carried him out the side door. His head hung down, nodding grotesquely with our movements. His arms dangled and I wished I had tied them. It all seemed unreal, dream-like. I kept my mind on details.

From the narrow strip in back of the house, we lowered him in the harness I had made at one end of the clothesline. He thumped along the face of the cliff, hung in air, disappeared. Then the line went slack and I knew he had touched ground. We fastened the rope to a tree above and I lowered myself, with the shovel tied to my back.

Now that the sky had become overcast, I could barely see. But I dug, stripped to the waist, with enormous haste and energy. The ground was soft enough but I had to clear small rocks and twining roots. Above I could see the feeble dance of Nancy's cigarette. I dug down and down, until I read the first glimmer of day in the sky. Then I heaved the body in and covered the sight of it.

I tamped the earth smooth. Too late I remembered the possessions in his pockets. Letters? A wallet? Money? What difference? Nancy had lowered his suitcase, unopened. And that, too, was buried with him.

I tied the shovel to me and pulled myself up. Nancy said nothing. I undid the rope and we went back into the house. Nancy had been busy. She had already cleaned the mess on the parquet floor. We looked around. Everything was as before. But for canned images of him on reels of film around the country, Norman Rainey might never have existed.

Again, Nancy and I stood looking at each other. "What did you do with the knife?" I said.

"I washed it and put it back in the drawer."

"Let me see it."

"Why?"

"I must know every detail."

. She shrugged and led me to the kitchen. From a drawer she removed a bone-handled carving knife with a thin narrow blade about six inches long. It was spotless and shone evilly.

"Put it back," I said. "It's as good a place as any. Without a wound to match it, a knife is a knife."

In the living room, we stood looking down from the picture window. The beginning of dawn was a murky gray sky. But below, the tree and the patch of ground beside it were visible now. It seemed closer than in darkness. But without a sign that anyone had set foot upon it.

I wondered if Nancy would ever again be able to enjoy the view. Her eyes might wander, but they would always come back to the spot. And whatever her fame or fortune, she would have to live in this house. For years, if not a lifetime.

Right at that moment, with her eyes glued to the place, she said in a small remote voice, "You might not believe it, but there was a time I thought I was in love with him."

29

I studied her in amazement. "Nancy, if you were in love with him, why would there be any need for him to try to rape you?"

"Because last night I didn't love him at all. I really hated him." She held palms to her temples and squeezed, shutting her eyes. "Please, please! Not now. I don't want to talk about it. Or think about it. For just an hour. Just one little hour."

"All right."

"The hour will belong to us—not him."

I looked at her.

"It's raining," she said. "See, there are drops on the window."

There were.

"Will it make any difference—down there?"

"No," I said. "The hole is deep. And packed tight."

"Then I don't care. I love the rain. It's cozy. I want a drink, Glenn. A strong one."

"A while back you said you didn't drink much because it did terrible things to you."

"It makes me forget certain obligations to myself. Obligations I had when everything in me was fresh and new, no filthy handprints on body or soul. But that seems long ago now. Not even important. How about that drink?"

We had several. Fast. Downing them in near silence. Then she said, "I can't stand it. I can't stand these gloomy morbid thoughts. Say something!"

I couldn't think of a word worth speaking. There was too much guilt in me.

She got up from the sofa and fixed a record on a hi-fi set. Music swirled softly. "Dance with me," she said.

"No."

She shrugged and, out of rhythm, began a series of unconnected little steps around the room. Every now and then she would pause as if listening to something other than the music, then go on.

30

Suddenly she stopped, covered her face with her hands and let out one great muffled sob. But as I was rising from my chair, she dropped her hands and went on with that awkward, compulsive dance.

About the time I felt a shout rising in my throat, the music broke for a few beats between the change of selections and she poured a new drink, came toward me.

"I'm beginning to get beautifully drunk," she said. "Beautifully, beautifully. Maybe you never noticed, Glenn. But whenever you saw me drinking, it was just a little wine and ginger ale. Because way back I discovered that real booze has the oddest effect on me. I have all the inhibitions of a virile sailor after a month at sea. Drink doesn't just loosen my inhibitions. It washes them out as if they never existed. Isn't that awful?"

"Yes," I said, wetting my dry lips. "And no."

"Don't look so stern. I did it, not you."

"That's true," I reminded myself aloud. And felt the stirring of change in me.

"Hear the rain?" she said, listening, raising her head to the ceiling. "It's a nothing day. Nothing but rain. Rain and Spain and gain. And love. It's a love day. Nothing but love. Love until noon—lunch. Then love until six—supper. Tiring, isn't it?" She laughed. A little hysterically. She drank and jiggled to the music and drank. My eyes swept over her and held on the tips of breasts surging unconfined beneath an aqua sweater.

She finished her drink and hurled her glass across the room, where it broke wetly against the wall and tinkled on the floor. She giggled, said, "I've only made love willingly and completely to one man in my entire life. And he didn't love me. But you love me, don't you, Glenn?"

"Yes. Yes, I love you, Nancy."

She swayed over me. "Tenderly?"

"Tenderly."

"Violently?"

31

"Violently!"

"And we're partners? Silent, silent?"

"Silent."

"And lovers, lovely, lovely?"

"Lovely. Oh, very goddam lovely."

She whirled away from me and began to dance, now gracefully in time to a slow beat. As she came by she whispered, "Love dance," and pulled the sweater over her head without losing step.

The skirt came next, but with more difficulty. And then she was naked—but for panties frail as pink gauze. She danced closer and the intrigue of her dance was in the subtle insinuation of her movements.

Tiring, she came to a halt in front of my chair and slowly settled over me like a warm scented bath.

"We must escape, escape," she murmured in my ear. "Escape with me, darling. Hurry! There's nothing left in the world but escape. . . ."

Some measureless time later I came awake as though my eyelids were snapped open by springs. I was looking at the spread of Nancy's hair on the pillow beside me. One arm draped across me, she was asleep. The expression on her face was innocent as childish slumber after a day of innocuous little games. I took a moment to be sad before I saw sunlight attacking the curtains. That all-day rain had been only a shower. I sat up abruptly to peer at my watch. Twenty minutes before ten.

"Nancy, Nancy!" I shook her.

She came awake with a smile that faded, sneaked off her face with awareness. "What is it? What is it!"

"It's the same lousy world from which we tried to escape a few hours ago. Get dressed. Fast! It's late and there are still things to be done. Remember?"

"I remember," she said. "Oh God, I remember."

6...

The story first came to life in the newspapers three days later. And with at least one angle that was news to me—puzzling and shocking.

Meanwhile, I had stolen some plates from a well-demolished Ford, a new victim among a sea of others on a wrecker's lot. I changed these with the ones on Rainey's Lincoln, had the car painted black at a quicky joint I found out on Pico, and drove it to Long Beach, where I put it in storage. I had wiped the interior clean of prints and en route I wore gloves.

The shovel had been secreted in the trunk of my car and I returned it under cover of darkness. Rainey's .38 revolver was hidden away in my apartment. When I mentioned it to Nancy, she looked bewildered. She could think of no explanation.

During this crucial time, Nancy and I kept apart. It seemed wise not to be seen together for the first few days. Then we would date and appear to "find" each other. We kept in touch by phone.

But on the morning of the third day after that grim night, I found the paper, with the story that Norman Rainey was missing, outside my door. The details were slim. According to Marvin Grinstead of Grinstead Productions Inc., Rainey had been driving alone to the loca-

33

tion scene of a nearly completed Grinstead Western in Nevada. He had not arrived on schedule, but at first it was presumed that he might have stopped off in Las Vegas to visit friends. A check indicated that this was false, and a private search was begun. When Rainey did not show after two days, the matter was reported to the police. And then came the shocker.

Rainey had been carrying a large sum of money for deposit in a Vegas bank. The money belonged to Grinstead Productions, in which Rainey had considerable stock, and was largely intended to meet the huge payroll for the cast and crew on location. It was almost certain, therefore, that Rainey's disappearance indicated foul play. An intensive search and investigation was under way.

The minute I read this bit of news, I began to have serious doubts about Nancy. I called her immediately.

"Nancy," I said, "did you read this morning's paper?"

"Yes, Glenn, I read it."

"Well?"

"I know you're not going to believe me, but I don't know a thing about it. I never saw the money and he didn't mention it."

"Obviously he had it with him, Nancy. There are a lot of things you never got around to telling me and I don't care for this new development one little bit. I think we ought to have a talk."

"When?"

"Now."

"No, listen, Glenn, why don't you wait until—"

"I'll be there in twenty-five minutes." I hung up before she could give me an argument. The phone was ringing as I went out. I didn't answer it.

Nancy's cliff house, as I came to think of it, looked, in the clean burst of morning sun, the picture of innocence. A place where jolly friends played bridge and exclaimed over the view, risking nothing more dangerous than a cocktail. Pink stucco, flowers, a picket fence in the sun.

She opened the door before I reached it and closed it as if a mountain lion were dogging my heels. She wore a wool-knit suit of turquoise. Her face was drawn; there were puffs of fatigue beneath her eyes. Even so, she managed to keep me in awed silence for the first few moments. Immediately she crossed the room to the liquor cabinet and poured herself three fingers of bourbon.

"I never used to touch this stuff at all, let alone in the morning," she said. "Now look at me. Drink?"

"Thanks. Not for me." I went over to the picture window and looked down. The landscaping above Norman Rainey was unchanged.

"I tried to ring you back, Glenn. You shouldn't have come."

"They, whoever they are, might as well get used to seeing me around." I sat down.

"You may find out all too soon who *they* are. Anyway, I'm glad to see you. You can't imagine what it's like, alone in this house. If I don't get out of here—"

"Nancy, don't stretch this thing called love too far," I said.

Sitting on the sofa, she drew her long legs beneath her. "What do you mean?" she said to her glass.

"I mean that if Rainey was leaving directly from here for Vegas . . ."

"He had the money and I killed him for it?"

"That would be another game. One I won't play, for love or anything else."

"Not even for half the money, darling?"

"Not even for all—with the darling thrown in."

She looked hurt, then stern. Seconds passed while she stared at me with level eyes.

"I've fallen a long way from my own shiny conceptions," she said. "But not that far. I didn't know he had the money with him, before or after it happened. I wouldn't want any part of the money even if I knew where to find it. And I don't."

It was easy and necessary to believe her.

"If you don't know, then I think I do," I said.

"Where?"

"It must be buried with him. In the suitcase. And that's why he was carrying a gun."

"We've got to find out," she said.

I nodded.

"Why, oh why, didn't we look?"

"At the time it didn't seem important to know what kind of clothes a dead man was taking with him. It's a repulsive thought, but I'll have to go down there to-night."

"And if you find the money?" she said.

"Nothing. It stays with him. Because you can't turn it over and say, look, fellas, I found this dough, but please don't think I know anything about dear old Norman Rainey. He just told me to keep it for him."

"How about some anonymous method?"

"You double the risk. They could trace it down. Let them think he was killed for the money on the road, and his car stolen. Or that he just took off with it, never to be seen again."

"Oh, what a mess, what a horrible mess," she said. "If Marvin Grinstead or the police get one little clue, they'll never leave me alone. The police, certain members of the police, will want that money almost as badly as Marvin."

She gave me a darting look, reached for a cigarette.

I stood over her with the light. "Strike that note again for me, Nancy. It went a little flat. Why should the police be interested in the money—other than recovering it for the owner?"

Smoke drifted from nostrils as dainty as fine crystal. She plucked a shard of tobacco from the moist tip of a fiery little tongue.

"In my mind," she said, "the money connects with a very dangerous situation. More slimy and fantastic than anything yet exposed by the scandal mags. And at least two members of the police department have more than a dutiful interest."

"I want to hear about that, Nancy. And everything else you left out."

Nancy was listening. But not to me. She got up suddenly, went to a front window, and looked out, then turned to me with a face that might have been struck by an open hand.

"Don't try to guess who just pulled up," she said. "I'll tell you. It's Marvin Grinstead."

"What am I supposed to do? Hide in a closet?"

"Just prove you're an actor. Old friend on a casual visit. I'll do the talking." The bell chimed and after a decent delay, during which she kept wiping her hands on her skirt, trying various expressions, finding the coolest in her repertoire, she opened the door. Not very far. I couldn't see him.

"Hello, Marvin. What do you want?"

"Now what would you guess, Nancy? I want to come in." A gray voice, deep and flat, edged with weary aggression.

Nancy stepped back.

Enter Marvin Grinstead. A man not far beyond forty. Middle-sized, but burly as a weight lifter. He had sparse sandy hair. His features were heavy and creased with the inroads of hard living and hard knowing. He looked like a man of ponderous thoughts, all of them cynical and vindictive. For all this, the eyes behind steel-rimmed glasses seemed deceptively apologetic.

His brown tweed suit was rumpled, though I'm sure he didn't know it. He seemed like a man walking a narrow track toward an invisible but certain destination.

He came softly to the center of the room, saw me, accepted me like the rest of the furniture.

37

"An old friend of mine from television," said Nancy. "We used to meet each other walking on and off. Glenn Harley—Marvin Grinstead."

I rose and he shook my hand, laying his on top of mine the way you might give a tip to a bellboy. Not disdainful, just disinterested.

"You're an actor?" he said to a point over my right shoulder, and walked toward that spot.

"That's right. An actor."

"Everyone in Hollywood is an actor," he said to Norman Rainey, some fifty-six feet below the window where Grinstead had come to rest. And that was the last word he spoke to me. I became an unseen spectator.

"Well, Nancy," he said, without turning from the window, "what have you been up to?"

It was one of those meaningless questions in which the guilty see vast undertones. Coming across the room, Nancy did a little skip, as though she had been reminded that she was out of step, then continued on blandly, fell upon the sofa, reached for a cigarette, lighted it.

"I read the paper this morning," she said.

"Oh?" He turned. Just his head. Looking back over his shoulder. "What do you make of it?"

"At first I thought Norm might have gone off on a drinking spree. But then when I read about the money. . . . Is it true, that part?"

"Uh-huh. It's true."

"How much?"

"Three hundred fifty thousand."

"My God, isn't that the amount you—"

"The full amount." He turned away from the window. "The entire payroll. So then, Nancy, when you read about the money, what did you think?"

He moved near her, hands behind his back, craning his neck forward. "What did you think?" He seemed sincerely interested in her reaction.

"I thought he might have been hard pressed. He lives

38

like a millionaire, and he's always up to his chin in debt. I thought he might have vanished on purpose."

"Nonsense, nonsense," he said in the same hard-soft voice. "I thought you were a smart little girl. When you got a face like his, a walking billboard that says, I'm Norman Rainey, picture star, you don't dare get lost. Not on purpose. Not on your own purpose."

"A foreign country?" Nancy reached for her remaining two fingers of bourbon on the coffee table.

"Nah. Even there. Besides, he was moving up, had a share in the business, stood to make more in the long run. And he had an ego big as a whale, the kind that had to go on seeing itself screened. Anyway, you think he would cross me?"

"I don't know. How should I?" She sounded cool.

"You should know, Nancy. You should know."

She gave him a look that would cut diamonds.

"So then, if he didn't run with the money, what do you think happened, Nancy?"

"I think someone did him and the whole world a favor. Someone got rid of him and took the money." She swallowed more bourbon.

"Who?" He leaned toward her intently.

"Maybe one of your little friends, so-called."

"Sure, but which one?"

"I have company, Marvin. Please get out."

He straightened, took off his glasses, pinched his nose, wiped the lenses with a handkerchief. "We're going to find out," he said. "We won't miss. I have help on both sides of the law."

The glasses went back in place and he walked deliberately to the door, opened it. Nancy remained seated with her back to him.

"By the way, Nancy. You didn't see Norman in the last three days, did you?"

She didn't answer.

7...

"**H**e was looking right down there," said Nancy, when we heard Grinstead's car pull away. "Right at the spot." She had been perfectly composed in his presence, but now her hand trembled as she lighted still another cigarette.

"He was just looking," I said. "At the view. Be careful not to put a false interpretation on every action. You'll go to pieces."

"You're right, of course."

"But I will say you appeared calm, Nancy. In fact, you were brusque. You might at least have told him you didn't see Rainey."

"I tried to act the way I always act with him—somewhere between indifference and loathing. He should know better than anyone that I stopped having anything to do with Norman Rainey. If I had been coy with Marvin he would have been suspicious."

"If Grinstead wasn't suspicious, why did he come here in the first place?"

"Well," she said, "my guess is that he's just sniffing around in every possible corner. He's probably been everywhere else and this is a last resort."

"All right," I said, sighing. "It's about time I got the whole picture. Why did you hate Rainey?"

40

She sighed. "Must you know?"

"Yes."

She held up her glass. "Get me a refill, then."

"You shouldn't drink so much. You need to be thinking clearly."

"Please, Glenn. For this I need courage."

I gave her a short one and after she had downed it in one desperate gulp she said, "It begins with Marvin. I blame him almost as much as Norm. He's a ruthless operator. And that's all he is—an operator. He never has any hard-earned money of his own. But he has connections. So he borrows. Or swindles, in one of his many con games. He uses underworld methods to get himself into more or less legitimate business."

"Underworld? Is he associated with it?"

"He was schooled in it. But I don't know his whole history. Just a few things I heard. Prostitution in Las Vegas, an interest in a new Vegas gambling club that now is going broke. I heard that once he had call girls and bookmaking operations here in L.A. Before he went into the nice clean business of making quicky films with dirty money. In a nutshell, Marvin Grinstead is a guy who wants to make millions in pictures with everyone else's money—borrowed, stolen or otherwise."

"And where do you come in?"

She got up, went over to the window. Looking down, she shuddered visibly, turned away. Finally she began speaking in a low voice.

"Marvin offered me a part, one night at a party. If you can call it an offer. He was gassed and he didn't bother with subtleties.

" 'How are you fixed for work, Nancy?' he asked. 'I'm not,' I answered. We were dancing in a crowd of monkeys, all pushed together, and he was using it as an excuse to wear me like another suit of clothes. 'And how about money?' he said.

" 'Fresh out,' I answered.

41

" 'I've got a bit part for you,' he said. 'It should be worth about twenty-five hundred. Don't be in a hurry to sign. Think about it. I'll put the contract under the pillow and we can sleep on it—together.'

"Just then we were passing a serving table. I reached out and picked up a great big highball. 'Here's to it,' I said. And threw the liquor in his face. While he was wiping himself off I told him what I thought of him in loud, clear tones. The whole room had stopped to watch and listen. There were a lot of snickers. He was publicly deflated and terribly angry. 'I won't forget, you phony little virgin bitch,' he said. 'I'm gonna fix you—fix you good!'

"And he did. Because he owned Norman Rainey and he knew I was pretty far gone for Norman. So he got Norman, whom I soon discovered never loved anyone but himself, to ask me to marry him. And I went for it. There was a license and a wedding with two witnesses—Marvin, who had apologized profusely, and one of his yes-men. And there was a minister. Only the license was a fake and the minister was an actor."

"Good God, what then?" I said.

"The honeymoon was in Marvin's cottage at Lake Arrowhead. I had finally allowed myself a few drinks, and I was uninhibited. Oh, very! Norman wouldn't turn out the lights because he said a body like mine should never be in darkness. He said a lot of obscene things which I rationalized as passion. Oh, grand passion.

"A week later, Grinstead had us over to his house to see what he called a preview of a new picture. Meanwhile, I might add, the alleged marriage was kept secret because Norman said he was going to build me as a star opposite him and I would be more exciting if at first it was believed I was single.

"So we sat there in the darkness of Grinstead's projection room and he flipped a switch and the picture, sound and all, came on. The first thing I saw was myself—taking my clothes off in a bedroom, with my dear husband standing out of camera range. It was a lewd feature starring Nancy Rhymer and Norman Rainey—please excuse his back being to the camera."

"No!"

"Oh, yes. That little cottage was wired and lensed for action. And you can't imagine with what fascination your chaste friend here, the sweetest girl in town, watched that action. Until I screamed for them to stop it and the lights went on and Grinstead proudly announced his and Norman's little joke."

Nancy lowered her head and began to cry, softly. "But the joke wasn't over," she said, after stopping a minute to compose herself. "They used that film to get me into the filthiest racket ever to hit Hollywood. And when I decided not to kill myself after all, I thought, the hell with it, might as well get down in the muck with the rest of them and come up smelling of money. Except that I never would let Norman Rainey touch me again."

"No wonder you hated him," I said. "And Grinstead. The evil bastards! You might as well tell me the rest of—"

The phone was ringing. Nancy went to answer. I could hear her distantly. It was someone called Mary Ann. Mostly, Nancy listened. But when she spoke, there was new tension in her voice. She said something about giving her ten minutes, and hung up.

I heard her rushing around. She came back carrying a pocketbook.

"I've got to go out," she said nervously. "I've got to meet someone. Right away."

"Who, for God's sake?"

"The name wouldn't mean anything to you. Mary Ann DeGraw."

"Why can't it wait, when there are so many things I should know? This is no time for play."

"It's not play." She moved to the door, dabbing at her hair. "Mary Ann is deeply involved in the whole mess.

43

Something has developed and we've simply got to talk. Make plans."

"For what?"

"A way out, I hope." She opened the door. "For me, anyway. Mary Ann should be happy with her lot."

"You're speaking in riddles. Why should she be happy?"

"Because she's a complete nymphomaniac."

I waited for Nancy to smile. She didn't.

"Nancy, what, for the love of God, is it all about?"

"It's about the greatest game ever invented for extorting money from people who have lots of it. I'll tell you later."

"The hell with later! I don't want you to go."

"If you don't want to wait," she said, "come back about three." She opened her purse and gave me a key, which I took reluctantly. "It's a spare," she said. "In case I'm late. 'Bye, Glenn."

"Nancy!"

But she was skipping toward her car. And when she backed out furiously and drove away, her eyes were fixed straight ahead. She looked frighteningly determined.

44

8...

Half an hour later I was in a hardware store on Santa Monica Boulevard, buying a shovel. It seemed too risky to borrow the one in my building again. I had them wrap the shovel, and went out the back door to an alley where I had parked my car. I placed the shovel in the trunk.

Next I drove to an ad agency on Vine. I waited a half hour to see a producer. He gave me two minutes in which he smiled, nodded approval, told me what a good actor I was, then said he had nothing for me, and went out to lunch.

I nosed the Chevy into the carport of my apartment house on Franklin and climbed the stairs. On the way I passed two men coming down. They squeezed in to let me by and I gave them a long glance.

They were strangers. Dressed in drab business suits—a little too drab for most callings in casual Hollywood. They had height, about six feet apiece. And a bulky look. They were somewhere in the mid-thirties, though one looked younger, with his blond brush-cut, his round, freckled features. The other was dark, with bushy brows. His face was long and sharp—nose, cheekpoints, chin, were spikes of bone. He had a skin that would never look well-shaved.

45

Though they spoke not a word to each other, there was a feeling of unity about them, a paired forcefulness. Coming down, their eyes never touched mine, and this gave me a chance for study. On the other hand, their turning away from me seemed an unnatural avoidance.

I had an unreasoned conviction that they had just come from my apartment A hunch. But a strong one.

I opened my door and stood for a moment looking around the miniature living room. Nothing seemed out of place. Neatness is almost a fetish with me. Physical disorder gives me a sense of mental confusion. I like to be able to put my hands on any possession instantly and without a ridiculous search. Thus, if so much as an ash tray were moved from one table to another, I would notice.

I went into the cubicle of a bedroom and began to open drawers. Not an object appeared out of position. And still there was an uneasiness in me that whispered of change.

It came to me then. In that cramped space there was a faint odor of fresh cigarette smoke. While I had been gone for hours, and was not then smoking.

In one stride I had the closet door open and was pulling down from a shelf two shoe boxes in which I kept a camera and photographic equipment. Beneath the gear in one of the boxes there was a square of cardboard which made a false bottom. When I pried this up I was glad I had taken the pains. Rainey's stubby .38 was there. I replaced the boxes.

A study of the clothes on the rack was revealing. I keep my clothes in sections, according to type. And I face them in the same direction. A sport coat in the center of its section had been returned in reverse order from the others. And below on the floor, one shoe was just enough out of step in the row to be noticeable.

I went downstairs and rang the super's bell. As he opened the door and recognized me, I had the impression that his eyes made a slow retreat into the shade of self-concealment.

"Just wondering, Mr. Lubke," I said, "if a couple of friends of mine came around asking for me? I told them I might be late and that you would let them in my apart-ment. I thought you might have sent them away."

He had the face and neck of a turtle and now both came out of the shell. His eyes widened.

"You were expecting?" he said. "Friends?"

"That's right. Two big guys. A blond one and a dark one."

He pulled back into the shell and peered at me with a dull groping in the arid desert of his intelligence.

He shook his head. "No," he said. "No guys come here. But I could give a message."

"Never mind, Mr. Lubke. They've already got the message."

I began calling Nancy Rhymer at three. I had decided to make sure she was home before I went up. At first I called every ten minutes, then every half hour. When night had sneaked into my living room like an enemy and she still hadn't answered, I stopped pacing and hurried downstairs to my car.

Pushing into the darkness, up the same hills, around the same angry curves, I wondered if she was there and just not answering. Was there any particular reason why she told me to come at three and didn't mention calling first? And in God's name, why were those two guys searching my apartment, and who were they?

The house was dark. I parked in front, then changed my mind and backed into the carport where the Chevy wouldn't draw attention. From the glove compartment I took a small flashlight I'd bought that afternoon.

I used the key Nancy had given me to open the front door. Inside, I had an overwhelming urge to flip switches and flood the place with light. I restrained it. I didn't want to advertise my presence to anyone passing by.

47

There is probably no gloom so thick with morbid suggestion as the gloom of a house in which there has been murder. A chair, a table, a mere lamp, outline themselves in darkness with grotesque forms. The quiet is enormous, the atmosphere smothering and oppressive.

I let my eyes adjust a few moments, then pulled the drapes. Cupping my hand over the neck of the flash, I flicked the switch and followed the narrow ray around the living room. I cut the light and went toward the bedroom. Entering, I again allowed my eyes to adjust.

My attention was drawn to the bed. There was a shadowy ridge of form at the center, as if someone lay there, drawn up into a ball, in the position of a fetus. I moved in a few steps, paused. I gave the bed a quick shot of light, just a wink. And sighed. Nancy had not made the bed. A blanket and coverlet lay rumpled together in the middle.

I moved around, closing blinds, went back to the living room, remembered the bath. But it was empty, also.

In a kitchen drawer, I found the coil of clothesline. Carrying it, I went out the side door, fastened one end of the line to a tree. Then I got the shovel from the car and tied it across my back.

Visibility from a three-quarter moon was good enough, and slowly I let myself down the cliff to the ledge with its lone tree. I took off my coat and tie, inspected the ground and began to dig. The newly shoveled soil was even softer than I had imagined and my progress was rapid. I came to the broken tangle of roots and knew I was almost there.

I paused to look above and to listen. A little late. In my haste I had forgotten. But there was neither sound nor light. I began to dig again. No more than a foot to go.

At what I believed to be the exact depth I found a gold tie pin. But two feet, three feet deeper, and that was all I did find. Occasionally chancing a light, I dug

48

frantically in every direction. But the body of Norman Rainey, his suitcase and every evidence of him were gone. Except a tie pin.

There was no time for speculation. With great heaving strokes I covered that hole, tamped the surface, grabbed coat and tie and hauled myself up with the shovel.

I restored the shovel to the car and the rope to the kitchen. Panting, bathed in sweat, I sat on the sofa, just above the spot where Norman Rainey had poured his blood on the floor. Beyond the window, flung to the horizon, the night was a garden of flowering lights. Behind every light I saw treachery.

Only one other person knew where Rainey's body was hidden. With three hundred fifty thousand dollars. Nancy had told either Grinstead or the police. But if she had told the police, why weren't they swarming over the place? And then I remembered that Nancy spoke of certain policemen being in league with Grinstead.

In any case, Nancy had involved me in murder and robbery, then left me to play her hand out alone. I had to find her!

The hell with the lights! I turned them on. The L. A. directory was under the phone. I thumbed through for Mary Ann DeGraw.

No listing.

I spied a desk and windmilled my way through papers, letters, albums, knickknacks. Nothing. I went into the bedroom and ploughed into a welter of frilly garments in more drawers. In a vanity I found what I was looking for. An address book. It was full of names. Some of them famous.

And then there was Mary Ann DeGraw. An address in Santa Monica. A phone number. But it seemed unlikely that I would get much information by calling. Strange voice on a phone. Better to persuade in person.

I dropped the book in my pocket, doused the lights and slammed the front door behind me.

9 . . .

The apartment house was on a side street several blocks removed from Wilshire in Santa Monica. It was a street darker than most and I had difficulty finding the number. Every now and then I would have to stop and check with my flashlight.

The building was a long, gray-blue L with white trim. Amber lights at the base of palm trees gave it a look of dreamy splendor. Through an arch I could see a courtyard and the underwater luminescence of a swimming pool.

The overnight parkers had taken all the space. I had to go around the corner for one of my own. I came back and began the hunt for Mary Ann DeGraw's apartment. I found it at the end of a third-floor breezeway overlooking the pool. I brushed a last remnant of Coldwater Canyon dirt from my trousers, straightened my tie and pushed the bell button.

The door opened to the limiting extent of a brass chain, and a vague slice of female face became outlined.

"Yes? Who is it?" Suspiciously.

"I'm looking for Nancy Rhymer, Miss DeGraw."

There was a silence. "Nancy isn't here. But who are you?"

"A friend of hers—Glenn Harley. She was supposed to

50

meet me at her house hours ago. I got tired of waiting."

"What made you think she was with me, Glenn?" The voice had dropped its guarded tone and became warmer.

"I was there when you called her."

The chain rattled and the door opened.

She was tall. Her hair was the color of dark walnut polished with a wood-lover's hand. It fell sinuous and casual down one side of a face composed in lines of languid grace. A young face, wise but without hardness. In the misty lavender of the eyes and around the lazy spread of mouth, there was a look of beckoning toward some erotic dream of which she had a sly and special knowledge.

Beneath a turquoise hostess gown, it was clear that she had the figure for marvelous dreams.

"Why don't you come in," she said, stepping aside. "As you see, I wasn't expecting company."

I moved past her into a living room which would have swallowed two of mine. It was a place of feathery-soft divans, hugging the floor and scattered with rainbow flufls of pillow; of thick-pile rugs, Chinese lamps, mirrored walls. Vast chairs, oddly shaped, some of them big enough to hold two people. The lighting was dusky, the mood suggested the sensuousness of the Orient.

There was a faint odor in the air, foreign to anything I could think of.

"Nancy told me about you," said Mary Ann, closing the door and refastening the chain. "Nice things. Oh, very nice." She had a way of smoking up even a simple word like nice. I thought of what Nancy had told me about her—a complete nymphomaniac. I wondered.

She flowed toward me, her stride parting the curtain of her gown from the long rich lines of her stockinged legs.

"My roommates will be curious," she said. "Let's surprise them."

"Roommates?"

"Yes. I have two, you know. Lovely ones."

51

"Well, good. But I really must find Nancy."

"Come along," she said with a twist of a smile. "Plenty of time."

I followed her down a wide carpeted hall, right. Then left, passing darkened rooms on the way. She opened a door and we stepped into a bright bedroom.

The little brunette with the round child's face and pouty mouth sat before a vanity mirror, brushing her hair with rhythmic strokes and counting aloud. Eighty-six, eighty-seven, eighty-eight. . . . She wore only panties, and in the mirror I could see the lifting cones of her breasts.

The other, a cameo blonde with dancer's legs and proportions in the pattern of a Moulin Rouge chorus girl, stood naked in the center of the room. With a burgundy towel, she was drying the soft convolutions of her anatomy to a pinkish white.

The girl before the mirror stopped her counting, squealed and turned her little head with an expression that was merely scolding, as she measured me.

The blonde caught one end of the towel between her legs and slowly stretched the other to conceal the blooming of those wonders above.

"Mary Ann, you bitch!" she said. But without real anger and with the barest trace of a smile.

"Girls, I want you to meet Glenn Harley," said Mary Ann with social-tea politeness. "That's little Donna at the mirror, and in the latest in towels we have Nanette."

"Hi," I said weakly. It was one of those rare occasions when I believe I was actually blushing.

"Hello man, now *go*, man!" said Donna, hugging herself.

"So terribly glad," said Nanette, backing away. "Please be a perfect gentleman and take Mary Ann out of here and drown her in the pool!"

"It wasn't my idea," I said. "But you've been pretty sporting about it."

Outside, Mary Ann said, "It's these little informalities that make life so charming, don't you think?"

"That's what I've always said, Mary Ann."

"If everyone met coming out of the shower," she went on, "there would never be any Hollywood phonies trying to impress you with their importance."

"You have a point," I said.

I didn't give a damn what anyone did or said. I wanted to know about Nancy. And if it was necessary to play games first, I'd play them.

In the living room, Mary Ann stood before a table and opened a drawer. She turned. "Want a stick?" she said.

"Pardon?"

"Are you on tea? Do you smoke the happy weed?"

Then I got it. "No thanks," I said in a voice that tried to sound as if she had asked me if I took cream in my coffee. Anyway, I had come to a point where I was beyond shock.

Mary Ann closed the drawer and lighted one of her sticks.

"It's not my first tonight," she said. "I was puffing my way to joyland before you came." She sat beside me on the divan, drawing deeply. Immediately the foreign odor I had detected became clear.

"I have to talk to you about Nancy," I said. "But first, if you want to offer me something, how about a drink?"

I needed one badly. I needed several.

"Scotch or bourbon?" she asked.

"Bourbon—half a hand on the rocks."

She disappeared and returned with a huge glassful.

"Thanks." I drank. "And now, what happened to Nancy? She was to meet me around three this afternoon and didn't show."

She sat down again, crossed her legs with revealing daintiness and peered at me sleepily through a swirl of smoke.

53

"I haven't the foggiest idea what happened to Nancy after she left me."

"What time was that?"

Mary Ann took a puff to consider. "Oh, it was twoish o'clock, I'd say."

"Where?"

"We had martinis at the Beverly on Sunset. We talked for quite a while and then Nancy said she had to get home. She drove off in her car. I'll admit she was nervous. But really, sweet, why do you worry? She takes such very good care of herself."

"Did she mention meeting anyone—aside from me?"

Mary Ann tossed her head. "Unh-uh. She said you were the only one she could trust. Because you were too far gone to see anything but her wings."

"She said that?"

"That was the drift, my sweet."

Right then I was taking still another look at Nancy. She had no wings and I was her angel. Sponsoring a show in rehearsal for a surprise ending. One I had a feeling I wouldn't like.

"Mary Ann, what do you suppose happened to Norman Rainey?" I watched her closely to see if Nancy had told her anything.

Her face kept its dreamy composure. "You can't tell about that one," she said. "He wheels fast in all directions—especially down. And no brakes. Maybe he got on a gambling kick in Vegas and lost all those pretty green marbles. Then he couldn't come home. He got the big fear."

"Grinstead?"

"You hear things from Nancy, don't you, lover?"

"We have no secrets. She was giving me the wide-screen, stereophonic version of Arrowhead when you called."

"Norman and his honeymoons," said Mary Ann with a lazy, sardonic smile.

54

"Grinstead and his cameras," I said. "Recording everything for posterity."

"Don't think," said Mary Ann, studying the ash of her happy weed, "that Nancy is the only one. Many of us were launched to nowhere in Marvin Grinstead's honeymoon cottage at Arrowhead."

"You, too?"

"Me, too."

"I'd like to hear about that. When I find Nancy. You have no idea where she would be?"

"Drifting around," said Mary Ann. "Drifting in the sky with a guy. She'll come down."

I stood.

"Don't go," she pouted. "Stay here with Mary Ann, sweet. I have no wings. But I can teach you how to fly."

I looked at that velvet body stretched back upon the pillows. At the slow fire curling behind the lavender of her narrowed eyes. And I was tempted. But I was in tortured haste to find Nancy Rhymer.

"Thanks for the offer, Mary Ann. But before we can fly together, I've got to put in some solo time."

At the door she said, "Life is a great big scrambled juke box. And love is on the flip side of hate. Maybe Nancy's with Norman Rainey, wherever he is."

"Oh, God," I moaned. "You don't know what you're saying."

She leaned close to me. One hand toyed with the back of my neck. "I'll see what I can find out," she said, seriously. "I'll check around."

"Now you're talking sense, Mary Ann. I'll be in touch."

I went back into the night.

10...

From my place, I phoned Nancy again. Nothing doing. I got out her address book and began to dial insanely. I went through the alphabet. I even talked to a couple of Big Names who couldn't understand how I had their unlisted numbers. The response I got ranged from surly to indifferent. A dozen or more numbers didn't answer at all, and a servant-type said Grinstead was out and he'd never heard of Nancy Rhymer. It took a long time and it was a wasted effort.

I was about to ring Mary Ann DeGraw when I heard the door buzzer. Certain it was Nancy, I ran to let her in.

The two men who stood there were the same I had passed on the stairs. They had cool eyes and falsely polite expressions.

"Police," said the dark one with the sharp features. "I'm Santella and this is Detective Yeager." Santella gave a tilt of his head toward the brush-cut blond with the meaty, freckled face, then produced a wallet and showed his credentials. I had no doubt at all they were real.

"Like to talk to you, Harley," said Santella.

"What about?" I asked.

Santella's jaw worked slowly on a piece of gum. "You gonna let us in?"

I stood aside and they ambled into my living room, glancing about as if they had never seen it before. I closed the door.

"Mind telling me why you're here?" I said.

"Nope," said Yeager, the blond one. "We don't mind."

Santella took the wad of gum out of his mouth, worried it into a ball, looked up. "We think you killed Rainey," he said.

"That's ridiculous. I don't even know anyone by the name of Rainey." It was the best stall I could think of.

"You go to the movies, don't you?" said Yeager, standing spread-legged in the center of the room, squinting at me.

"Oh, that Rainey. Norman Rainey. Sure, I know of him. Who doesn't? The papers said he was missing, not dead."

Santella tossed the gum back into his mouth, pushed himself up from the arm of a chair. He walked casually toward the bedroom and spoke over his shoulder. "We'll take a look around—if you don't mind, Harley."

"You should know your way," I said. "But I haven't changed anything since this afternoon."

Santella turned, exchanged looks with Yeager. "This is a wise boy," he said. "I think he's gonna be trouble."

"Nah," said Yeager. "You just don't understand him. I figure he'll be easy."

Santella went on to the bedroom while Yeager remained behind. He sat down comfortably, fired a cigarette and watched me with a bored expression. Meanwhile, Santella drifted into the bathroom and later the kitchen. I could hear him opening drawers, banging them shut again, not really trying. I knew it was part of an act, but the reason for it escaped me completely. I was plenty worried. I had felt doomed from the moment they came in.

Santella returned, said, "What did you do with the money after you killed him, Harley?"

It didn't deserve an answer.

"Where do you keep your car?" said Yeager.

"Below. In the carport."

"Let's have the keys," said Santella.

I got them out of my pocket and tossed. Santella missed and they dropped to the floor.

"Pick them up," he said.

I stood there. I knew just enough about cops to be certain these weren't playing by the book. I was afraid and angry at the same time.

Yeager came up behind me and gave me a shove that sent me sprawling to the floor. "Pick up those goddam keys!" he said.

I got up and the keys were by my foot. I kicked them across the room. "Try that again, you bastard," I said to Yeager, "and I'll bust your face open." I meant it.

Yeager whipped his gun from its holster and advanced.

I caught his wrist as the gun barrel came slashing down for my temple. I held on and clobbered Yeager in the eye with my free right. He jerked back and his wrist slipped from my grasp. He recovered quickly and had the gun trained on my chest in an instant.

I could see by his narrowed eyes and twisted mouth that he was out of control. He was going to kill me. I dove for his legs and he went down with me. The gun fell from his hand and I was reaching for it when he punched the side of my head with such force it hurled me off him onto my back.

We both came to our feet at the same moment. I was cocking another right when an arm closed around my neck from behind. It was Santella. He pulled me to the floor. Yeager stepped over and kicked me in the groin. He kicked me twice more in the ribs. Then, when Santella let go, he stepped down hard with his big foot on my windpipe. The foot sank deeper as he gave it more weight. I felt my Adam's apple being slowly crushed.

I choked, stopped breathing. The room hazed out.

Santella said something sharply and the pressure went off. When I looked up, Yeager was kneeling above me, holding his .38 like a club over my head. He was drooling at the corners of the mouth, his face distorted. He was mindless with rage.

"I'm gonna beat your face in, Harley," he sobbed. "Bone by bone."

The butt came down and I swung my head aside. The gun struck the floor and while he was off balance, I gave him a mighty shove and leaped up. Santella had his own gun on me before I could move.

"That's it!" he barked. "The play is over. You too, Mike. We need this guy in one piece. So just can it! We're wasting time." He crossed, picked up the car keys.

Yeager hesitated, then put the gun away. "You'll learn some new tricks tonight, friend," he said. "You'll learn manners when we get you in a cell."

"C'mon, c'mon!" said Santella. "Downstairs." He gestured for me to precede. I went out the door and led them below to the Chevy under the building. It was dark.

"Wall switch is over there," I said, pointing. I knew they would find nothing in the car.

"Never mind," said Santella. He took a flashlight from his hip pocket, tried a key in the door. "Don't work," he said, and tried another. The door opened. He climbed inside and flashed over and under the seat, inspected the glove compartment. "Clean," he said. "What's in the trunk, Harley?"

I remembered the shovel! "Nothing," I said. "Just some tools."

"Okay," Santella said. "Back upstairs."

I began to move ahead of them. I couldn't believe I was that lucky or they were that stupid.

"Hold it," said Yeager. I stopped. "Why should we believe this guy? The money could be in the trunk."

59

"Yeah," Santella answered. "Maybe we should have a peek, huh?"

They took me back.

"Which key?" asked Santella. His mouth worked easily on the gum. Under the soft deflection of light from the flash his face was an etching in bone.

"The round key," I said. No use to stall now. Not much they could do about a mere shovel.

Santella bent over, got the key in the lock, turned. He gave the handle a wrench and pulled up.

He was a moment bringing the light to focus and I guessed before I saw the interior. The fetid breath of decay seeped out of the trunk. The wretching, sick-sweet odor of old death.

"God!" moaned Santella.

"Damn. Oh, damn!" said Yeager.

I didn't say anything. I just stared at the rotting, naked body of Norman Rainey.

11...

Santella had the suitcase open on a chair in my living room. It had been right next to the hunched body of Rainey.

"Nothin' in here but a mess of moldy clothes and a bottle of Scotch," he said to Yeager. "Whud you do with the money?" he snapped at me.

"I don't know anything about Rainey or his money," I answered. I wasn't lying about the money. Not now.

Santella smiled. "No? Rainey was just walking around in his skin. Carrying a suitcase and a shovel. He broke into your trunk, closed the lid and knocked himself off. Right?"

"Let's see what he's got in his pockets," said Yeager. "Put your stuff on that table, Harley. And don't miss anything."

Except for one small item my fingers touched, I emptied my pockets. But Yeager ran his hands over me, found it, held it to the light.

"Now why would Harley want to hide a little thing like a tie pin?" he said. "Don't make sense. Until you see this monogram—initials N. R. Norman Rainey."

"Geez!" Santella said. "The janitor down at City Hall could convict this guy." He went through the rest of my things on the table and gave them back to me. He shoved me into a chair, leaned so close I could see the gold fillings in his teeth mashing gum.

"You stink, Harley," he said. "Already you stink of gas. Cyanide gas. That's how close you are to that little green room where they'll use it on you. Twelve years with the force and I never knew a guy who was caught with such a neat bundle of evidence.

"I figure a jury will be out about ten minutes. Just to make it look good. And then the foreman will stand there in that quiet courtroom and he'll say, 'Guilty! Guilty of murder in the first degree!' After that you'll sweat a few months in a cell on the Row. Yeah. How you'll sweat. And then one night they'll come and get you and they'll strap you into that chair and they'll drop the cyanide pellets into the acid, and a couple of minutes later you'll be one very dead sonofabitch."

He paused, unwrapping a fresh stick of gum. Taking the wad out of his mouth, he folded the new stick around it. His jaws opened and the glob went back into the grinder.

And I thought, he's right. I'm tied to that body and no one will ever believe me. I might as well have been caught in the act. Nancy's act. I needed time to hate. And time to think. And there wasn't time for either.

"Now let's see what we have here," continued Santella. "We've got Rainey's body in the trunk of your car. And his suitcase. And a shovel to bury him with. A nice new shovel. And in your pocket we find his tie pin. Now all we need is three hundred fifty thousand bucks. Whud you do with it?"

"I'll tell you once more, Santella. I never had the money, never set eyes on it. Rainey's body was planted in my trunk."

"Is that right, now? And the shovel? And the tie pin?"

Ask Nancy Rhymer, I wanted to say. But something held me. Maybe the uselessness of accusing her. I was silent.

Yeager took off his coat, began rolling up his sleeves. He came over. "You're gonna cough up money or blood, you sonofabitch."

Santella waved him off. His bladed features tried to look soft. And almost made it. The gum settled into a lump under his cheek and he spoke confidentially, as if to a small boy in trouble.

"Now look, fella. In a couple of minutes we put the cuffs on you and we take you in and book you. It's a big haul for us. Lot of glory, you know. We get our names in the paper. We get a citation from the old man. Maybe we make sergeant. Week or so later it all dies down and what have we got? A piece of paper says we're good bright boys and there's a few bucks extra in the paycheck. Buys a few more cans of beans. You think that's enough for us?"

"Depends on how you look at it," I said, trying to see what he was driving toward.

"Yeah," said Santella. "It depends on how you look at it. But suppose we don't like beans. Suppose we like fat steaks and luscious dolls. And the crinkle of hundred-buck bills back to back. And we say to you, 'Glenn boy, you tell us where that dough is and we never heard of you. We don't know what's in your car. That's your business. You got somethin' there you wanna hide, well then you take a long ride somewhere and you hide it.' And you never see us again. And this slob Rainey stays on the missing persons list. They never find him. See what I mean?"

I saw. With intense clarity. The whole filthy scheme. And I had an idea.

"I might play ball with you guys," I said. "What choice have I got?"

"Smart," said Santella, touching a finger to his brow. "Smart."

"But first I have to know one or two things myself."

"Like what?" said Yeager, moving in again.

63

"Like who told you where to dig up the body?"

They looked at each other. And smiled.

"Was it Nancy?" I still couldn't bring myself to use her last name.

Santella went on smiling. "You got hot pants for the wrong baby, my friend," he said. "But we don't know anyone by the name of Nancy. Not even if you said her last name was Rhymer." His smile lingered.

"Thanks," I said. "I'll remember. For a long time. I suppose she told you the money was in the suitcase."

"Maybe. Or maybe when she found it wasn't there, she needed a little help, in fact, she needed a lotta help." He smiled, knowingly.

"Well, Harley, what about it?" said Yeager. "You want out or don't you?"

"Damn right I want out. But how do I know you won't cross me as soon as you have the money?"

"You don't," Santella answered. "But it's the only gamble you've got left, buddy boy."

I pretended to look thoughtful. "All right," I said. "The money's in a locker. I'll get the key and take you there."

"Sweet damn, now you're talkin'!" said Santella.

I got up and began to walk to the bedroom.

"Where you goin'?" said Yeager.

"To get the key."

They followed me, watched as I brought down the shoe box.

"We looked in there," said Santella.

"You still missed it," I said. "Under all this gear." I tilted the box toward me so they couldn't see. I fumbled under the junk, as if searching. Meanwhile I lifted the false layer of cardboard, got my fingers around the butt of the .38 and came out with it fast and level.

I've never seen two more astonished faces.

"Back into the living room!" I ordered. They moved warily in front of me. Santella had a look of indecision.

64

"Hands on top of your heads where I can see them," I commanded. They obeyed.

I stood by the front door. I wanted to relieve them of their guns but I felt it was risky. Santella looked dangerous. His face was too calm and knowing. Then again, I could try one of their own methods.

"Turn around and face the wall," I said. "Arms out and lean against it. You know how it's done, so don't give me any crap!"

I had in mind taking their guns and my car keys from behind. The car keys were all-important. And there had to be two sets—or how had they got in my trunk with the body?

Yeager turned around and began to move to the wall.

"Hold it! Hold it, Mike," said Santella. "This guy is no hood. He won't shoot a cop. I got him pegged." He came slowly toward me, lowering his hands.

"One more step and you're a dead cop, Santella!"

But I wasn't so sure. I was confused. It never occurred to me that I would meet resistance. And since basically I was innocent, I wasn't going to kill. I only wanted to get away.

Santella took that step and I hadn't fired. Gaining confidence, he came on slowly. Yeager had turned, looking puzzled but still wary. My hand reached back and touched the doorknob.

"Give me the gun," said Santella. His hand was out, as to a savage dog that can be placated with persuasion. His mouth moved perpetually around the gum. I tried to watch him and Yeager at the same time.

Suddenly he took two long strides and was on top of me. I belted him with a left to the jaw that carried a hundred and ninety pounds of steam. He went down. Out of the corner of my eye I saw Yeager reaching for his gun. I hauled the door open, heaved it shut behind me just as the first shot ripped wood and sang around the hall.

65

I crashed down the stairs, stumbled, recovered, fell mightily at the bottom. The .38 spun out of my hand and across the floor as two more shots whipped down from above, chipping cement a foot from my head.

I crawled out of range, got to my feet. Shoe leather pounded the stairs. Someone shouted. I ran into the night.

Outside, a few people were coming out of doors, calling to each other. I saw heads duck back as another shot flew after me and missed. I zigzagged around a corner, cut across the street into an alley between two apartment buildings. The alley went nowhere. I was boxed. I looked back. They had seen me and were thumping after me. Too close.

I saw stairs leading to a basement. I scuttled down them. There was a door. It was locked. I heard Santella and Yeager come to a halt just above. I crouched back and down into shadow.

"This alley dead-ends," gasped Santella. "Bastard must be right around here."

"Shoot the sonofabitch," said Yeager. "Kill 'im!"

"Stairs over there," Santella said. "Where's that goddam flash? Got it!"

Light touched the top of the stairs. I felt for the gun, realized I had lost it. And that was a time I would have used it. For I knew they would kill me.

Then, in the overspray of light, I caught sight of a broken pane in the door. I eased up, put my arm through, felt a bolt. I slid it back just as the light began walking down. I turned the knob and slipped in, fell prone. It saved my life. A slug smashed glass where my head had been a moment before.

I was up and running. The basement of the apartment building was dark. But huge and uncluttered. I saw a distant light and pistoned toward it. I found myself in a wide hallway. There was an elevator. The door was closed. I looked around frantically. Stairs! I hurled myself above.

66

I reached the first floor, went out the front entrance, clipped down the walk. At the curb a teen-ager was just grinding the motor of his hot-rod jalopy to life.

"Police!" I shouted. "Burglar getting away. After him!" The kid's mouth fell open. I ran around and got in. "Take off!" I hollered.

We scooted away, burning rubber. Behind us on the walk, I saw Santella and Yeager, raising guns.

"Which way, which way?" the kid said breathlessly.

"Around the corner and back toward Sunset!" I shouted above the roar. "Look for a gray Hudson."

The kid stole a sideways glance at me.

"Where's your pistol?" he said.

"Right here in my holster, son," I said.

"I thought I heard shots," he said excitedly.

Trees, houses and blocks flew by. The kid was good at the wheel. We came to Sunset. I heard sirens. "Go right," I said. "Right!"

We made the turn on a yellow. Rubber squealed.

"How do you know he went this way?"

"Slow down," I answered. "I think we lost him."

"Damn!" the kid said.

I spied a little restaurant with an awning and a French name. I told the kid to stop. I jumped out.

"Thanks anyway," I said. "Good try. I've got to phone the station." I ran into the restaurant.

I looked out. When he had gone, I went back to the street. The kid might talk to the wrong people.

I walked quickly west for several blocks until I came to a dark little bar. Inside I found a phone booth. I got out the address book and dialed.

"Mary Ann?" I said.

"Who speaks, my sweet?"

"Glenn Harley. Mary Ann, listen to me! Don't move out of there. Just wait for me. I'm in trouble and I've got to find Nancy. You're the only one in this whole godforsaken town who can help me now. Don't fail me!"

12...

I had the cab driver let me off at another bar —on Wilshire in Santa Monica. A new thought had come to me. Feverishly I dialed Mary Ann.

"I'm right around the corner from you," I said. "But I want to talk to you alone. What about your roommates?"

"Resting from the strain and pain of this cruelest of all worlds. In their little beds."

"You didn't say I was coming?"

"They're asleep."

"And tomorrow morning, if anyone asks, you must say you never saw me again. Right?"

"I am silence. But why do you beat your wings, my pet?"

"Mary Ann," I said sternly. "This is serious business. Do you think you could come down out of the clouds long enough to help?"

There was a space while she considered. "I never can face realities for more than an hour at a time," she said in an entirely different tone. "You may consider me grounded for an hour."

"Good! Now look, have you a car?"

"Yes."

"I think it would be better if you picked me up here,

then. Do you know some out-of-the-way place where we could talk in privacy?"

"I could take you to a place that was built for privacy." Her voice dropped as she said it, drew a picture of exotic intimacy.

I told her where to find me. "Can you make it in ten minutes?" I asked.

"I'll be there, Glenn. But I don't like mysteries. Will you give me a hint?"

"I'm about to be crucified. I'm dead if I don't find Nancy Rhymer. Fast! Did you check on her?"

"Everywhere. And unless she's on the moon . . ."

"In ten minutes then, Mary Ann. Make it less. Hurry!"
She clicked off.

It was called The Sheik and was shaped like a miniature castle, loosely Arabian style. It was north of Sunset on a narrow country-like road in the vicinity of Bel-Aire—not a section in which you would expect to find a nightclub.

During the drive a squad car came out of a side street, and instinctively I ducked down. That was when Mary Ann became nervous. That was when she refused to go on unless she knew why I was hiding from the police. I figured she wasn't going to get out of my sight to inform on me. And I needed her. There wasn't another soul who might make clear to me what kind of racket was behind the whole terrifying mess. Or lead me to Nancy. So I told her. Everything.

I didn't care what happened to Nancy. Not now. I didn't understand why she had framed me, unless to cover herself. Or for money. It didn't matter. I hated her more fiercely than I had loved her. I was going to find her before the police found me. And, by God, she was going to confess!

For once Mary Ann came out of the smoky dream world in which she existed. She was genuinely shocked.

Even sympathetic. I could tell right away she knew Santella and Yeager and was in terror of them. I was questioning her about them when we drew up in front of
The Sheik and went inside.

A big twilight room gaudily dressed in someone's idea
of a harem. Tables with dim electric candles. The bartender wore a turban and the waitresses were in sleazy
costumes with bare midriffs.

Mary Ann ignored the main room, crossed it to a door
beside the bar. She waited until she had caught the bartender's attention. He gave her a tight nod, there was a
thin buzz and click, she opened the door and we
mounted stairs.

"The bartender has a little button he presses," explained Mary Ann, as we climbed.

The second floor was, if possible, darker. Same decor.
There was another bar with another turbaned tender
but there were no customers at the bar. A dark-haired
hostess in costume greeted us.

"A booth, Miss DeGraw?" she murmured.

"Of course, dear," said Mary Ann.

We moved across the room to a row of curtained
booths. The curtains were red velvet. Many were drawn
tight. The girl paused at one and stood aside for us to
enter. Two long red-plush divans faced each other. They
sat low on the floor and were separated by an ebony
table. A shielded electric candle was the only light.

Mary Ann sank upon one of the divans and pulled me
down beside her.

The girl stepped in and said, "Would you like to order
now?"

"A fifth of bourbon, ice, and water," said Mary Ann.

As the girl departed, Mary Ann turned to me. "All
right with you? This way we won't be bothered again."

I was so nervous I didn't care what we drank. "Even
moonshine a day old," I said.

Mary Ann's smile jeweled the darkness for an instant,

70

then flicked out. Her face became grave. She crossed her legs and adjusted a silky black skirt. She wore a gold dress-sweater sequined with silver and her white breasts proudly soared from the half-moon dip of neck-line.

"Rainey dead," she said in a hushed voice. "I can't believe it. And Nancy . . . I never knew that one very well. She mingled but she didn't mix. She never pretended to be one of us. She was just too big, too good."

"Was? Why do you keep saying was—as if she were . . ."

"Dead? Listen, it's possible. With this crowd, it's possible."

"No. I don't believe it," I said. "She'll be hiding until I'm snug in jail."

"Oh, the bitch! Selling you out like that. After you saved her neck. Rainey deserved what he got. But she would have gone to jail."

"Hold it!" I hissed.

The girl had returned with the order. She set glasses in front of us, a carafe of water, a bucket of ice and the fifth. When she had gone, Mary Ann drew the curtains tight and sat down, leaning forward, holding her head in her hands as if in a torment of her own. She no longer seemed the sex bomb Nancy had painted her. At the moment, I wasn't even curious.

"Mary Ann," I said, "I know you're involved in some phase of this thing. Nancy told me that. And I don't give a damn. I'm no moralist. I have no ax to grind. I was shoved in a hole and I want out. Maybe you're in a pit of your own. We can help each other, if you tell me what kind of a lousy game this is. Starting with detectives Santella and Yeager."

She looked up, frightened. Brushed a nervous hand down the long drape of walnut hair. And was silent.

"Forget it, then," I said, standing. "Just forget it. I'm in a hurry. I can't sit here sucking my thumb. Not while

71

the whole goddam police force of Los Angeles is out looking for me. But remember, you haven't got any more friends than I have. These boys play rough. When Rainey's murder comes to public light, maybe a lot of other slime will get some airing. And then you just imagine to what lengths boys like Grinstead, Santella and Yeager will go to cover it up. They'd throw you to the wolves. They'd stop at nothing."

She grabbed my sleeve. "Sit down," she said. "Give me time to think. And then we'll talk. . . ."

13...

I fell limply beside her and she began pouring heavy slugs over ice. We drank deeply. A long time passed before it helped. The thumb of my right hand kept twitching in little spasms. I saw police cars roaming side streets, fingering searchlights into the shadows. I heard sirens. And the clack of teletype machines sending out their all-points bulletins. And I saw the hungry, determined faces of Santella and Yeager.

"C'mon, c'mon!" I said. "I'll give you a start. Extortion. Some kind of sex blackmail. . . ."

Slowly she nodded her head. I knew she was going to tell me now. It was important to know it all. Because somewhere in the sewer of truth, there was a clue to Nancy.

"How did you find out that much?" she said.

"Nancy. But she never had time to finish it."

"It's gone too far," she said. "I should have known . . . But I couldn't help myself. I got trapped the same way Nancy did. Except with me, Rainey didn't have to use that marriage gag. I was a model trying to sleep my way into pictures. And when Rainey invited me to the cabin at Arrowhead, I went willingly. Nancy told you how they take these . . . these dirty films in that sneaky way. They threatened to show them at smokers attended by the big shots, send a copy to the police, mail stills to every producer in town. And the newspapers and—"

"If Rainey was in the pictures, wouldn't he be incriminated?"

"Oh, no. They were too clever. They never showed his face. Only mine. And the others."

"What others?"

"The girls you met tonight are two of them, Donna and Nanette. Misery loves company. We all live together."

"And what was the purpose? To make you enlist in some pornographic film-making on a big scale?"

"Worse. And much more profitable. There is a certain element of movie stars, producers, directors who can't get enough kicks. They have all this money and they're restless. They want to buy thrills. They want parties—Roman style, when Rome was one big orgy. They want playgirls for these parties who aren't cheap floozies with worn-out bodies and faces to match. And we were the chosen ones. Of course we got paid. Very well. But there are things you don't do for any amount of money."

"So the gang collected money from these Names," I said. "And they paid you a fraction. Where do Santella and Yeager come in?"

"Grinstead and Rainey weren't satisfied with the take. Rainey was a flop, even in B-pictures. His contract had been dropped. He was down and going broke—until Grinstead took him in and offered him a small share. Grinstead himself was operating on a shoestring and desperate for money. So they cooked up a beautiful cross with Santella and Yeager, a couple of shakedown boys on the vice squad."

"All right. What was the gimmick?"

Mary Ann opened her cigarette case.

"It was so simple, my dear. And practically foolpoof. In the middle of this latest and greatest orgy, at the most compromising moment, Rainey gave a signal and Santella and Yeager came in through a back window. With them were a couple of Grinstead's flunkies playing reporter and photographer. Pictures were flashed and everyone was made to stay put at gunpoint."

"But the girls knew it was coming?" I said.

"Of course. We knew it wasn't a real raid. Well, not only was everyone running around like Adam and Eve in the garden, but also one or two of us were smoking tea, and some horse and needles had been planted. It was made to look like the worst kind of jam a Name could ever get himself into. Career ruined, a jail term, filthy publicity."

"So they paid and paid," I said. "How did it work?"

"Santella said he was going to call a wagon to take all of us in. About that time, Rainey suggested that the whole thing could be ironed out then and there if Santella and Yeager would listen to reason—spelled m-o-n-e-y. There was a lot of fake protesting and haggling. Finally, of course, they gave in. But only for fifty thousand from each of the victims."

"And they got it?"

"My dear boy, they got all of it! Everyone was held right there until morning when the banks opened. Then, because he was spokesman, it seemed logical for them to allow Rainey to make the collection. The sucker would have to write his check, then call the bank and say Rainey would be down for the money and it was okay to give it to him. Yeager went with Rainey, and when he phoned Santella that all the money was in, the Names were allowed to go free. And, of course, no one dared to talk."

"Grinstead was completely in the background?" I asked.

"Always. Rainey organized the party and pretended to be a victim."

"Just one party?"

"So far. I mean, of that type with the fake raid. They

75

were planning another. That's why I called Nancy and got together with her. To talk it over."

"Where do they hold these parties?"

"The last one was at Nancy's house."

"When?"

"The night before Rainey disappeared."

"And how much was the collection?"

"Three hundred fifty thousand."

"I'll be damned! That explains it. The missing money was not payroll—it was the goddam blackmail take."

"I was sure of it the minute I read the papers," said Mary Ann.

"So if you knew it, Nancy also knew it," I said. "She hated Rainey to begin with. But the real reason she killed him was to get the money. We'll assume that he told her he was carrying it with him. Afterward, she had no one to turn to. Certainly not Grinstead or any of his clan. Not Santella or Yeager, because they each expected a cut of the three hundred fifty thousand. She couldn't handle the body alone. So she called the prize goat of them all—lover boy Glenn Harley."

While we had been talking, Mary Ann had lighted one of her sticks. There was the sick-sweet smell of marijuana. Her eyes had narrowed and she seemed to lapse into character.

"My sweet," she said now, "you are a lamb shorn by the knife of love. Standing at the gates of the slaughterhouse. And I guess I'm not far behind."

My mind racing, I ignored her. Thinking aloud, I said, "Now I've got to take it a step further. Nancy must have found the money and hidden it somewhere. And all was quiet and peaceful. Until what? Until somehow Grinstead smelled out the truth. With the help of Santella and Yeager, he grabs her and forces an admission. A partial truth. Because she must have said that I helped her cover up and that if there was any money, I found it in Rainey's car and kept it. Obviously they believed her.

She applauds on the sidelines while they set about to kill two birds with one body. They can frame me and get her off the hook. And they can use the evidence to make a deal with me."

"Clever, clever," said Mary Ann sleepily. Her face had returned to languid sensuality. She poured me another drink. Was that my third, fourth? It didn't matter. My twitching thumb was now still.

"Of course," said Mary Ann, "it might be that she was telling the truth about the money. She didn't find it but pretended that you must have."

"What would be the point?"

"She stalls, my pet. Until she has a chance to look."

"My God, but where?"

Mary Ann only smiled and puffed. As if the last of sensible thinking had gone up with the smoke of her reefer.

"If Nancy didn't find it," I said, "there's still one possibility. And if I had that money . . ."

Mary Ann wasn't listening. She seemed to have lost interest. But not in me. She looked at me in a strangely enveloping way.

"If you're not going to help, I'm leaving, Mary Ann."

"On foot? I have the car, remember? So don't rush me. Now tell Mary Ann what she can do to save you."

"You can drive me to Long Beach," I said.

"And then?"

"Nothing. Just leave me where I tell you. And go home. You might get a call from me. On the other hand, you might never hear from me again."

"I'll take you," she murmured. "When I finish my joy smoke and get to know you a little."

"Now!" I said. "Take me now. I have no time for this."

"Relax, sweet. One for the road." She poured a drink and I downed it. What the hell, she couldn't be hurried. And she had the car. I let the bourbon warmth take hold. Grinstead would know where Nancy was. Santella and

77

Yeager also. They could be watched—and followed. They
might be persuaded. There were ways. Meanwhile, who
would find me here? I sat back, and some of the tension
seeped out of me.

Mary Ann languished on the divan. Her eyes were long
narrow slits.

"Never hurry to trouble," she mused. "Fun goes so fast.
And trouble goes slow. It creeps along and takes for-
ever." She studied her stick. "You take one of these and it
reverses the process. Trouble is a silly bubble racing
away on the wind. Gone. And fun—fun just drifts across
a pink sky like a lazy cloud. It's in no hurry to leave you.
Slow, slow."

She leaned close to me. "Do you like fun, sweet?"

"I never have time for it any more," I said.

"You should make time. You should learn to shift
gears in a storm."

Her hand dropped to my thigh, made little caressing
motions. She began to hum.

"Heaven," she sang, "I'm in . . ." She broke off.
"What did Nancy tell you about me, sweet? Did she say
I had a yen for men?"

"She said that you . . . I don't believe Nancy, anyway.
Why don't *you* tell me what makes you tick, Mary
Ann?"

I took another drink. It was a relief to feel and not
think.

"I don't tick," she said. "I soar. And I do have the
man habit. I'm incurable. I have no shame about it. I
have no shame about anything I do of my own free will.
People are boring themselves to death, lying with sugar
smiles about what jolly joy it is to do what everyone else
says is fun—good, clean, Sunday-school-picnic fun. Not
me. No one asked us if we wanted to come into this
world. And we had a dirty trick played on us. Because
we were born to die. We came in crying and we go out
crying. And, in between, all our laughter has the hollow

78

sound of the end. So I don't let anyone tell me what's heaven and what's hell on this earth. This is one kitten that knows she's condemned. Meanwhile the condemned cut herself a hearty slice of life and was never afraid to gobble it all up."

Her head fell on my shoulder. Her hand slid off my thigh and into my lap, paused. She kissed my ear, lingered there. "And what are *you* afraid of?" she whispered.

"Afraid you'll stop," I said against the moist spread of her lips.

"I couldn't," she answered, falling back, taking me with her. "Not for a long, long time," she said beside me. She took my hand and guided it beneath the sweater to the warm shock of bare breast. "Feel my heart," she said. "I'm a fast train on a down track to nowhere. And my heart says, couldn't stop—wouldn't stop—couldn't if I would—wouldn't if I could . . ."

And we didn't.

14...

"There's a drive-in on the next corner, Mary Ann," I said. "You can drop me there."

We had sliced through the darkened center of Long Beach on the main highway. It was ten minutes before one A.M. On my instructions, Mary Ann had driven at a moderate speed and in strict obedience to traffic regulations.

"Why won't you tell me," she said as she parked in front of the restaurant, "why you had to come way out to this dreary burg at one in the morning?"

"Sorry I can't explain now, Mary Ann. But thanks for the lift. And ... everything else."

"And after all the ... everything else, pet, you still don't trust me?"

"I have never found the ... everything else ... a guarantee of silence." I had the door open and one foot on the curb. Already I was eager to be gone.

Mary Ann laughed. "I suppose you're right. Or everyone over sixteen and under eighty would be mute."

"Good-bye, Mary Ann. And luck to you. If I ever get out of this jam ..."

She slid toward me. "Won't you at least call me?"

"I've got to go."

She kissed me and held on. I pulled away gently. I

did not want to hurt Mary Ann. She was one of the lost ones on the same road to oblivion all of us are traveling. But like so many escaping in the labyrinth of sensual amorality, she had more heart than guile, more warmth than a host of virtuous pretenders I have known.

"Go home and pack your bags," I said. "Steal away. Just disappear. While you still can. That's the best advice I've got."

I climbed out and closed the door.

"Too late for me," she said. "Remember, you've got my number, sweet. And where will you be?"

"Nowhere," I said. With a wave, I walked quickly away.

From the telephone booth outside the drive-in, I watched Mary Ann U-turn and fade north. Then I searched in the classified, found a cab company and dialed.

A five-minute ride and we had pulled up before the twenty-four-hour garage. I paid the cabby. The big sliding door was closed. I went in the small one with the glass window.

A great barn of a place with more space than cars. Two floors, with a ramp leading above. A gasoline pump and, next to it, a small cluttered office. I entered.

The lone attendant was stretched in a rickety swivel chair with his feet on the desk. He was reading a detective magazine with a lurid cover depicting a busty girl in a torn slip, shrinking back from the monster who was attacking her. The magazine came down slowly, but the feet remained.

"Yes, sir?" said the attendant. "What's yours?" He was young—late twenties—but nearly bald. He was big and going to fat. His nose was vast and he had a sloping chin and small black eyes that were sullen with the annoyance of interruption.

"Mine is a car," I said, producing the check. "I want to take it out."

81

He extended a fat ham and I dropped the check into it. He gave it a glance. Yawning, he got up and searched a rack until he found a mate. As he studied the matching check, I had the uneasy impression that he was no longer bored. His back was to me but there was a stillness about that great hunk of flesh.

When he turned, there was a wary smile on a face that wasn't made for smiling. The eyes were shrewd and alert.

"What kind of car you got here, mister?"

"Lincoln Continental. Black sedan. How much?"

Pudgy fingers counted each other. "Eight bucks, seventy-five," he said.

I had the exact amount and gave it to him.

"It's on the second floor," he said. "You kin take the stairs back on the right, or haul up the ramp. Keys in the switch. Can you find it okay?"

"You find it okay," I said. "That's your job, isn't it?"

"Yeah, well sure. But I'm alone tonight. We got a guy sick." His face tried to apologize but he was a lousy actor.

"I'll watch the store," I said.

He shrugged and went out.

I heard him coming down the ramp in a minute. He made a tight turn, gunned over and braked. He cut the motor, jumped out.

"Open that door," I said. "I'm in a hurry."

"You want gas? Better fill 'er up."

"No gas. Just open up."

"Got to check the tires," he said.

"Never mind the tires."

"It's a rule, mister. We never let no car's been sittin' this long outta here without we check the tires. Hold it while I hunt the gauge."

I started to object but he was striding into the office.

From my position I couldn't see the interior of the office. So I got out quietly, sneaked over to the little

82

cashier's window and looked in. He was seated at the desk, pulling a phone toward him. He dialed rapidly.

A few quick strides and I was standing there looking down at him. When he saw me, his mouth twitched and he dropped the receiver back into the cradle.

"Some jerk with a wrong number," he muttered.

"Funny, I didn't hear it ring," I said.

He frowned. "Now where did I put that goddam gauge?" His fingers drummed on the desk, slid away toward a bottom drawer.

I leaned over the desk fast and slammed a fist into his face. He spun around in the chair. I gave him a shove that sent him crashing to the floor, bellied over the desk and opened the bottom drawer.

It was a hunch with a big dividend—a .45 automatic. I had it cocked and trained on his face when he got to his knees and began wiping blood from the corner of his mouth.

"Don't bother to get up," I said. "Now, who were you calling?"

He looked at me dumbly.

"C'mon, c'mon!" I said. "You'll be a dead hero."

He flicked his tongue over his bloody lip, said, "The police."

"What police?"

"Couple of plain-clothes guys from L. A. were down tonight. They give me a number to call if anyone come for the Lincoln. Said the car was stolen."

"How did they know it was here?"

"They phoned all the garages, trackin' down a black Continental sedan. They had the motor number."

Sorry I forgot to tell you what garage, Nancy, I thought.

"What did these guys look like?"

"Big bastards. A blond shave-head and a dark man."

"And when they found the car, what did they do, check it over?"

"Yeah, I suppose. They wouldn't let me hang around."

I glanced about the room. At the far end there was a door with a lock.

"What's behind that door?" I said.

"Storage. Auto junk."

"Open it."

He blinked up at me. "Boss has the key," he said.

"Don't give me that. Open it!"

He rose like an elephant in a swamp, fumbled in his pockets, came up with a ring of keys. He lumbered to the door and opened it.

"Toss the keys on the floor," I said.

He obeyed.

"Inside," I said.

It looked like a frail door and he would splinter it with his weight sooner or later. But it would keep him off that phone just long enough.

When he was locked away I found the button to raise the huge electric door, leaped into the Continental and shoved for the highway as fast as it was possible to go with every police car in the state of California a potential enemy.

15...

Twelve minutes after three A.M. I had arrived at one of the few places they might not think to hunt me.

Nancy's house was dark—like all the others on the way up the hill. No cars around. Carport empty. I drove on past, circled and returned, lights out. I swung the Lincoln up the drive and into the port. I opened the front door with Nancy's key, went in behind the .45 I had taken from the garage attendant.

I got the flash out of my pocket and gave the room a spurt of light. The curtains were drawn—just as I had left them. But out of the corner of my eye I saw the desk. It was not at all as I had left it. The drawers were yanked out and turned over on the floor. With light and gun I moved through the rest of the house. It was a mess. Closets gutted, drawers emptied, mattress overturned, pots and pans strewn over the kitchen floor.

Someone had decided that Nancy might have the money after all. For just a moment I stopped hating her. Long enough to remember what Mary Ann had said—that she could be dead. That with this crowd it was possible. It was a rotten thought. I couldn't carry enough hate for her to want her dead. I pushed the idea out of my mind and got busy with the next problem—the reason I had gone out to Long Beach for the Lincoln.

If Nancy didn't have the money hidden and if it hadn't been found with Rainey's body, where else could it be but in some secret space in the Lincoln? There was an outside chance. And that three hundred fifty thousand had suddenly become important to me. In my situation, it would have many uses . . .

I began, as a matter of course, with the interior, up-ending-seats, lifting rugs to inspect floorboards, groping behind the dash. Nothing there. I wasn't surprised. Probably Santella and Yeager had gone that route before me. But my guess was that theirs was a merely routine check, since they thought I had the money.

Next I made a fruitless search under the hood. And finally I took off my coat and slid beneath the car. Using the flash, I made an inch-by-inch examination of the undercarriage. There were a dozen places where a box could have been fastened. They hadn't been used. I crawled out and brushed myself off, put on my coat.

Then, as a mere gesture, I again opened the trunk. It was clean of everything but a spare tire. And some tools; bumper jack, lug wrench and a tire iron. I closed the lid and went back into the house.

Exhausted from the strain of the night, I sat down in a chair, lighted a cigarette. I had time to be sorry for myself. If there was a lonelier soul on earth, I couldn't think how he got that way. I was up to my scalp in trouble, framed within whispering distance of the gas chamber, ten feet from a phone and not a human being in the entire city of Los Angeles whom I could call to lend a hand. My so-called friends of the playacting world would be ridiculously ineffectual. I was on the wrong side of the wrong police and Nancy was clueing the enemy to find me. Mary Ann was a junky, her loyalties unknown. I couldn't really trust her. And to add to the pain, of the only friends I could trust, those long green ones, there were just seven left in my wallet.

It was so pathetic I heard myself chuckling. The sound

86

was mirthless and not quite human. I choked it off.

I had to have money to move about. I began to wonder what I could sell, not caring if I owned it. Parts from the Lincoln? Radio? Spare tire? Tools?

My mind sifted these objects, weighed against them. Even if I knew where to sell a radio and a tire, there would be questions. A jack and a lug wrench? Hah! Three or four bucks. A tire iron? Worthless.

Tire iron. . . . A picture of it sat unwanted in my mind—nudging. Why would there be a tire iron among the tools? It wasn't standard equipment. Just a wrench and a jack. Most people didn't remove their tires from the rims of their wheels. No need to. They simply traded the spare for the faulty shoe, wheel and all.

I jumped up and went out again to open the trunk.

As I had expected, the spare was a tubeless. After I let the air out I pried with the iron until the rubber came away from the rim.

I was right!

The money was in tight rolls, fastened with rubber bands. Thirty-five rolls of hundred-dollar bills, each wad worth ten thousand.

In the living room, I sat staring at the green pile at my feet and I thought, the hell with the whole goddam world! I had an army of three hundred fifty thousand on my side. First stop—Hawaii. Then the Orient—Japan, China. Or Europe. South America. A good actor with a wig and a new face out of the make-up kit. A phony passport. Soft lights and softer dolls. Why, on that kind of money, just the interest alone . . .

If they wanted to play games, I could play, too.

I put the money in a shopping bag I found in the kitchen. And the shopping bag in a clothes hamper under some dirty towels. I kept a ten-thousand roll in my pocket. It felt good there. Bulging with security.

I was wide awake. With the .45, I sat down by a front window. To watch. And to think. And to wait for dawn.

16...

Even before the first wan light of day touched the sky, I had changed my mind. If I could prove innocence of murder, I would only be jailed as accessory in the concealment of a crime. On the other hand, having turned State's evidence, I would more likely go free altogether. It was worth one more gamble before I took flight and convicted myself by implying guilt.

I had a plan. I knew one thing for certain—I needed a base of operations. And this wasn't it.

After a short search, I found an overnight bag on the shelf of Nancy's broom closet. The color, powder blue, was far from masculine, but it would have to do. I covered the blue satin interior with the rolls of green, closed the case and locked it with the little key dangling by a string. I put the key in my pocket and I was ready.

A block from Fat Freddy's, a twenty-four-hour short-order house in Santa Monica, I parked the Lincoln in the private lot of an apartment building. They could have it. It was the hottest car in town. I was through with it for good.

Dawn was just becoming a reality when I walked into Freddy's, sat down in a back booth and ordered an enormous breakfast. I wasn't exactly hungry, but I had to have an excuse to kill a lot of time. The U-Drive-It place a block west wouldn't open until nine.

At eight o'clock, stuffed and on my fourth cup of coffee, I opened the morning paper which the waitress had just brought me by request. I spread the front page with a trembling hand.

At first I was amazed to find there wasn't a whisper of Norman Rainey's murder or, more important, a single line about Glenn Harley. Then it occurred to me that Santella and Yeager might want to conceal the crime until they got their angry mitts on me and the money. And that gave me hope.

Until I remembered those sirens wailing as we turned the corner in the hot-rod. Until I realized that it all happened too late to make the first edition.

At nine o'clock I was on tap as the U-Drive-It opened. I gave the clerk a line about being in a hurry because I had to meet a train downtown and my car was in the shop for an overhaul. I told him there was a ten spot in it for him if he could speed me on my way. I really wanted an excuse to make him pliable and not too exacting.

He protested the ten weakly, but I insisted. He stopped looking so sleepy, offered me a new Olds sedan, gassed up and ready to go. Then, almost apologetically, he wanted to see my driver's license. I flashed it in front of him so that he could identify it as a California license beneath the milky isinglass flap in my wallet, without reading it. I knew he would say that he had to copy the information—and he did.

I made a pretense of trying vainly to extract it, said, "Ah, the hell with it. I'll read the information, you take it down." He hesitated, saw the ten in his mind, nodded over the form. I gave him the name Ralph Barnett. Wally Barnett was a guy I knew in New York. I offered a phony address and faked two of the numbers on my license. All this in case the name Glenn Harley ever

89

sprang at him from the front page and he could then tell the police what car to hunt down.

I gave him fifty for a deposit and ten for himself, getting forty change from a hundred. I climbed in and took off. They wouldn't be looking for a gray Olds sedan.

Next I made a stop at a theatrical supply house. I bought a wig, make-up, glasses and other gimmicks of the trade—enough to satisfy Lon Chaney, Senior, in his prime. I paid for it with "expense" money from the Grinstead fund—which didn't belong to Grinstead. If the money ever got back to its rightful owners, they shouldn't kick about the loss of a few hundred for expenses.

I needed a shave badly and stopped at a barber. Then I paid a visit to a department store, where I bought two conservative business suits, with the provision that the tailor adjust the trouser cuffs to length while I cruised about, picking up shirts, ties, shoes and other accessories, including a brown leather suitcase and two large briefcases.

Dressed in one of the new suits, I made a final stop across from a gas station. Carrying one of the briefcases, now full of the paraphernalia bought at the theatrical supply house, I slipped unobserved into the men's john of the station, locked the door behind me.

When I came out I had aged a good twenty years. My light-brown hair had become mostly gray, with a seasoning of black. My skin was darker, with a mere suggestion of lines around eyes, mouth and forehead. My nose had been broadened. I wore horn-rimmed glasses and a mustache. I walked with a slight stoop. I was a middle-fiftyish man of no particular distinction.

It was not a burlesque. It was not a caricature. It was a subtle job which had taken a long time, while angry patrons hammered for entrance. As a layman I would never have tried it. But as an actor with a talent for make-up and dozens of character roles behind me, I felt

I had an excellent chance. Already my imagination was working the mannerisms of someone remembered, an old friend of my father's, into the part.

At the desk of the plush Palisades Hotel overlooking the Pacific in Santa Monica, I tried out my new manner of speaking. It was crisp—my own speech is easy. My voice is deep—I pitched it higher.

I signed in as Carl Dudley Quinn. A boy carried my bag to a room overlooking the ocean. I carried the second briefcase, which now contained the money.

Once I had hidden the briefcase away, I ordered lunch sent up to me. With a newspaper, latest edition.

It was now just after noon.

When the boy had set down his tray and departed with his tip, I quickly opened the paper.

There were two pictures under the black jolt of head-line. Norman Rainey's draped body in the trunk of my car. And off-center, just below, a fine likeness of me, with the caption, "Glenn Harley, murder suspect."

17...

NORMAN RAINEY FOUND SLAIN
ACTOR SUSPECTED

Those were the headlines. And the story was big. Very big. It continued on page two, with sidelines on page three. It gave Norman Rainey's history from the time he was weaned—a mawkish account, the false sentimentality which makes gods of monsters. And sells newspapers. Alive, Rainey was a second-rate ham. Dead, he was a Valentino enshrined.

My history was less detailed. Yet if I had known I was so "important" as a television actor in "key" supporting roles, I would have asked my agent to demand triple my fees. But, as the story went, my popularity had waned, I was apparently broke, and was suspected of having murdered Rainey for the money I knew him to be carrying. How I knew of it was not disclosed. It was hinted that I might have met Rainey in a bar on the night of his death and that he trusted me with the information that he was en route to Vegas to bank a three-hundred-fifty-thousand-dollar payroll. It was tacit that all actors of whatever stature or medium knew each other and traveled in the same circles.

The events surrounding the discovery of the body in my car were almost funny, as reported. Detectives

92

Michael Yeager and Anthony Santella of the Vice Squad had been investigating leads to dope users among "certain" show people in Hollywood. This in an effort to uncover the peddlers of narcotics. "Informers" had given them my name as a possible user, and they had come to my apartment to ask a few routine questions. During the course of the questioning I had pulled a gun from a hiding place and made my escape in a hail of bullets.

A tenant of the building had phoned the police, describing the scene as one of gangsters shooting each other in open warfare. Detectives from Homicide, led by Lieutenant Howard Purcell, had raced to quell the massacre, only to find Santella and Yeager with smoking weapons and empty hands. After a search of my apartment which disclosed nothing incriminating, Lieutenant Purcell had located my car. Finding the trunk locked, he had ordered it pried open and the gruesome discovery was made.

And, I thought, while the trunk was being forced open, there stood Santella with the keys in his pocket. The scheme had triggered too soon for him and Yeager. But I was the victim.

There was no mention in the paper of the hot-rod kid. And not a hint of Nancy Rhymer.

At the moment I was the most wanted "criminal" in America.

I went back to the picture of myself and studied it with grim concentration. It appeared to have been made from one of those glossy publicity shots which are on file in the offices of various producers, and had been taken several years ago. It was a flattering glamour-boy photo which inaccurately made me look something like Errol Flynn in his dashing, jail-bait era. It was overdone and underdone—washing from my face the character inroads of the lean, struggling years which followed its printing.

In the wrinkled sport clothes, badly needing a shave,

93

I did not think the clerk at the U-Drive-It lot would recognize me. And since he was the only one with a clue, I put the thought of immediate discovery out of mind and prepared to execute my plan.

I tossed aside the paper and grabbed the L. A. phone book. I thumbed through, found the number and wrote it down. Next I got the money briefcase from its hiding place and checked to see that it was securely locked. Then I went down to the lobby and had it placed in the hotel safe.

I hunted a phone booth, squeezed inside, dialed, asked for Lieutenant Purcell. I was connected with Homicide and a voice said Lieutenant Purcell was out but expected back in a short time. I waited ten minutes in the lobby and tried again.

I was informed the lieutenant was just then coming into the room. A weary voice answered, "Yeah, Purcell speaking."

"My name is Carl Quinn," I said, with my new, older sound.

"Yeah?"

"Give me a day or so and I can put you in touch with Glenn Harley."

"Is that right? You've seen him, have you? Well now listen, fella, so have two dozen other Joes who phoned in this morning. I haven't got time to run down every—"

"I have not seen him and I don't know where he is," I interrupted. "But I happen to know him and I've talked to him on the phone within the past hour."

There was a pause. "What's your name again, mister?"

"Quinn. Carl Quinn."

"All right, Mr. Quinn. I'm listening."

"The situation is this, Lieutenant. Harley says he's innocent, and I believe him."

"If he's innocent, get him the hell down here. He has nothing to fear."

"Nothing but the gas chamber," I said. "He won't be

94

down there at all. When he has a tight grip on the person who killed Rainey he'll call for you to come and pick him up with that person. He'll be in one helluva goddam hurry. So expect that call night or day, Lieutenant. And act on it. You're not talking to some crank."

"Give me your address, Mr. Quinn. And I'll hop over and have a talk with you." Restrained excitement was in the lieutenant's voice.

"Sorry," I said. "I'm just an intermediary. But I need a free hand. You'll hear from us."

I hung up before the long, complicated process of tracing a dialed call could be completed.

I went back to the room, phoned down for a typewriter. I got polite double-talk but I was insistent. A bellhop arrived in a few minutes with an ancient standard a little bigger than he was. I gave him two bucks.

When the door closed I got a piece of hotel stationery from the desk, tore off the letterhead neatly and rolled the paper into the machine.

It took me fifteen minutes to write for Nancy Rhymer her full first-person confession of the murder of Norman Rainey. The confession was simple and direct. It stated that Nancy Rhymer had stabbed Rainey with a knife when he tried to attack her and, although this was done in self-defense, she then became afraid the scandal would ruin her career and summoned Glenn Harley to help her dispose of the body. Harley had nothing to do with the crime directly or indirectly until it had become a fact. The body had been buried on a ledge below the house and was subsequently removed and planted in the trunk of Harley's car by persons unknown.

I had good reason for leaving out many other details.

I folded the paper and placed it in my breast pocket, called to order the typewriter removed.

The Palisades was a big hotel. It sprawled over acres of ground and had more than seven hundred rooms. Friends of mine had stopped there on occasion and I

95

had visited them. I had a pretty fair knowledge of the
layout. So that when I began to walk through the cor-
ridors, I knew what to look for.

First I spotted the stairs—about four doors down from
my room on the fifth floor. I climbed to the seventh
floor, swung right to the end of the corridor. Here, as I
remembered, was located a large corner suite facing the
ocean. There were two such suites on each floor at
opposite ends of the hallway. This one—709 and 710—
was reached by making a right turn at the end of the
hallway into a passage shaped like an inverted L. The
door to 709 was set in the long shaft of the L, while
710 was around the corner from it. I knew this only because a well-heeled pal of mine, an agency V.P. from
New York, had been there with a local cutie. The cutie
had a friend and we had quite a party in the suite.

I knocked first on the door to 709. When there was
no response, I tried 710. Sometimes a suite is sealed off
and the rooms are sold separately. But a fist on 710 got
only silence.

I took the elevator below and breezed up to the desk
clerk. "I'm Mr. Quinn in 522," I said. "I've just had a
call from some business associates who are joining me,
and I'll need more space."

"Yes, sir," he said. "What sort of accommodations
would you like?"

"Well," I said, "I once stayed in a suite here—709 and
710. Very nice. Is that available?"

The clerk consulted his cards and said that it was.

"I'm expecting three people," I said. "I'll move into
the suite but I'd like to hold onto 522."

"Yes, sir. What time will the gentlemen arrive?"

"I don't know. It may be very late, possibly not until
tomorrow. Under the circumstances, I'd like to pay at
least a night in advance for the extra room. The gentlemen will be my guests."

In ten minutes I was in the suite and again checking

the L. A. phone book. I had told the boy who brought me up that I was not ready to move my baggage from 522. In truth, I would not be ready to move it at any time. But I now had keys to three rooms.

I might have had trouble getting Marvin Grinstead to the phone. Except that I told the maid I was calling for Glenn Harley. Grinstead came on immediately.

"Who are you?" were his first words.

"Ralph Barnett," I answered. I had a reason for returning to the name I had given the U-Drive-It clerk. Principally, I didn't want Grinstead to find Room 522 if he ever inquired at the hotel desk.

"I don't know you, bud," he said. "Is this a gag?"

"It's no gag. I'm speaking for him."

"Say it, then."

"Harley wants to deal. That is, if you want your three hundred fifty thousand back."

"Don't be an idiot. Of course I want . . . But I don't deal with every bastard who climbs on my phone. Who the hell are you?"

"Watch it," I said. "Or there won't be any deal."

Silence. "On the level, you know where to reach Harley?"

"No. He reaches me."

"And what's the deal?"

"You know where the Ship's Anchor is—out on the pier in Santa Monica?" The Ship's Anchor had booths and was the darkest bar for miles around. I wanted to give my new face a first test in dim light.

"What's the Anchor got to do with a deal?"

"Be there at nine sharp tonight. Sit in a booth. And be damn sure you're alone. I'll find you."

I hung up.

Grinstead might only appear to be alone. But of one thing I was positive. He would be there.

97

18...

The Ship's Anchor was about halfway out on the Santa Monica pier, nestled among tackle-and-bait stores, a fish market and a hamburger stand. It was a restaurant and bar specializing in fish dinners and intimate ocean-view atmosphere after dark. There were two entrances—from the pier, and from the parking lot in back.

I entered from the parking-lot door about two minutes of nine. I stood just inside for a moment adjusting to the gloom and surveying the customers. There were less than a dozen people at the bar, a few dressed in fishing garb. I recognized none of them. The drinking crowd had mostly replaced the diners in the booths which ran along the two water sides of the room. I didn't see Grinstead, but from my position at the door the occupants of many of the booths were invisible.

I decided on a quick one to ease the tension. I stepped over to the bar and ordered a Manhattan. As the bartender moved off to make it, my eyes flicked up to the mirror behind the bar. I saw the reflection of a man who was standing very still and looking at me intensely. His hair was almost gray. He wore glasses, had a large nose, a strong chin and a mustache. He looked like a man in his fifties who was spoiling a still-decent figure with

98

hunched shoulders. Anyway, I didn't recognize him, but I turned to look. I couldn't find him. Until I turned back.

It was me!

I tried to sip the Manhattan but couldn't restrain the urge to hurry. I was getting nervous. So I gulped it down, paid and began to walk slowly past the booths, glancing in each one. On the other side of the room I passed a couple necking shamelessly, an empty booth, and beyond it, Grinstead. He was alone.

We looked into each other's eyes for a searching moment. I hesitated, went on to the end of the row, returned.

I leaned over the booth. "Are you Marvin Grinstead?" I said softly.

His eyes flicked over me; his nod was barely perceptible. I sat down.

He took a cigarette from a silver case without offering me one and, as he lighted it, his gaze over the flame was coldly appraising. I stared back at him, ordering my thoughts into discipline for the most important role of my life.

"Well, Barnett," he said. "It's your move."

"On the contrary," I said, listening to the high, tight clip of my voice with approval. "The next move will be yours." I took the typed confession from my pocket and passed it to him. "The money is ready and this is one of the conditions of the trade. We'll want the confession signed and copied just as written, all in Nancy Rhymer's own handwriting."

Grinstead said nothing. He removed his glasses and wiped them methodically with a breast-pocket handkerchief. While he did this, he stared at me continuously with a myopic squinting. He had a poker face that could play with the best in the back rooms of Vegas.

The glasses returned to his face and were adjusted with maddening deliberateness. Whereupon he held the paper this way and that until it captured enough light in the darkened room. He read swiftly, folded the paper, placed it in the center of the table and waited.

I had really expected that he would protest any knowledge of Nancy Rhymer in the first go-round. I was surprised.

A waitress came over and Grinstead shook his head. But I ordered a highball.

"There is one more condition," I said.

His lips pursed.

"We'll want the girl to bring the confession personally to a designated place, where she will sign it."

Behind the glasses his eyes drifted upward, his jaw worked around the thought. Watching him, I began to have some serious doubts.

"Of course you know where she is," I said.

He didn't answer.

"And she's in good health?"

He pulled a shard of tobacco from the mound of his lower lip. "Where did Harley find the money?"

"Rainey's car. Inside the spare tire."

He cocked his head—as if hearing the sound of the lost chord in the arrangement of his scheming.

"And the bills? What denomination?"

"All hundreds."

He leaned forward. "You have the full amount?"

"Minus five thousand for my cut as go-between. We guarantee three hundred forty-five thousand."

He didn't bat an eye. "How is it that Harley wouldn't deal the first time?"

That one caught me off balance.

"What first time?" I said finally. Only to see what he would say.

"I have no answers," he snapped. "Just questions."

"All right," I said. "He didn't deal the first time because he hadn't yet found the money. Your boys wouldn't have believed him."

100

"I have no boys, as you call them. I'm a businessman interested in the return of stolen funds."

"Fine," I said. "You stick with that. All we want is results."

He leaned forward again. "Who are you? Barnett? That's just a name."

"Don't worry. I'm no cop. So it doesn't matter."

"You have the money in your possession?"

"Of course not. You think I would risk my neck for five thousand?"

He actually smiled.

"And I don't have any more idea where Harley is than you do. I didn't want to know, for my own safety. So don't try to squeeze me. Because you've got no other route to the money, if I don't play."

"How do you get in touch, then?" he asked.

"He calls me."

"So we deal and he telephones you. Then what?"

"I tell him the confession checks okay. I put the Rhymer girl on and he talks to her for a minute. Just a minute. But he insists that no one else be present when he talks to her but myself. If he's satisfied, he sends a messenger with the money. You count it, you leave and I take possession of the girl and the document," I concluded.

"And what do you do with her then?"

"That's our business. We don't ask what you do with the money."

"What makes you think she'll go along with it? She has everything to lose."

"I think you could persuade her."

This was all talk on my part. I was expecting a double-cross and I was going to make it easy for them. But they would have to deliver Nancy Rhymer with her confession before they could cross me. My one sickening doubt was not *would* they deliver, but *could* they?

"All right," said Grinstead. "Where and when?"

101

"Harley wants to arrange the meeting in a hotel room."

"Why in a hotel?"

"Public place. He's afraid of a cross in some isolated spot."

"What hotel?"

"He'll let me know. I'll be in touch with you at six tomorrow night; we'll meet at eight. That should give you time."

"No deal unless I can bring a couple of men to guard Rhymer until we have the dough," said Grinstead.

I was expecting something like that.

"Okay," I said. "But they guard outside the door while she talks to Harley."

This was important. And he looked suspicious.

"I don't buy that," he said. "We step out and you lock the door."

"Wrong," I came back. "I don't lock the door and I give you the key. Besides, they only have to talk a minute."

He considered.

"Deal," he said. "If we have the key."

I pushed the confession toward him and he put it in his pocket.

"Until six tomorrow night then," I said.

He stared at me for a moment, then got up and walked out the door.

I sat there thinking it over, finishing my drink. It had been a strangely one-sided conversation and I was uneasy. Although I was nearly certain he hadn't recognized me, I had the lonely, frightened feeling of one guy playing against big odds. If my plan didn't work and I was caught, I would be safer in a cell awaiting trial for murder. Grinstead's agreement to the arrangements meant nothing. He would have a scheme of his own, whether he could produce Nancy or not. And if he couldn't produce her even to trap me, there seemed only one logical answer. She was dead.

102

And because even now the thought sickened me, I remembered what Mary Ann DeGraw had said. "Life is a great big scrambled juke box. And love is on the flip side of hate."

But there was one comforting thought. I would be watching for them to come. And unless Nancy Rhymer was with them, there would be no meeting.

I had drained my glass and was signaling the waitress for a check when I saw them at the bar. Santella and Yeager. Facing me, they talked together as if unaware. I knew they had been outside and Grinstead had tipped them off as he left. Even though I was prepared for some such possibility, the sight of them was a jolt. I ordered another drink to stall for an idea.

In the end I decided that under the circumstances their plan was only to follow me. But that was bad because wherever I lighted, they would stake me out. So I paid the check and sauntered toward the front door. There was a cigarette machine just beside it. I stepped out, pretended to change my mind and abruptly returned to drop coins in the machine. From the corner of my eye I saw that Santella was standing and Yeager was climbing off his stool. I knew they would not run and it would take them several seconds to reach the door when they made their move.

I put the cigarettes in my pocket and went out. As soon as I was hidden from view by the building, I sprinted around it and came in the back door. Of course, they had left.

I made for the men's room and ducked into a stall. leaving the door very slightly ajar. I sat down and pulled my feet up out of sight.

It was a full minute before I heard the door open, shuffling feet, silence.

"F'chrissake, I told ya!" Santella's voice. "Why would he sneak back here if he don't even know he's bein' tailed? C'mon!"

103

I waited a half hour, cramped and sweating. Then I peeked into the bar. They were gone. I went out the back way and climbed into the Olds. I locked the doors, closed the windows, put the .45 on the seat. I spun out the drive, heaved right and moved toward the exit.

In the mirror I saw lights swing from the parking lot driveway and follow. I knew it wasn't coincidence.

From the street above the pier, I made a quick turn and wound down to the Pacific Coast Highway, heading north and picking up speed. They made the same turn but had lost ground. They didn't waste time catching up, and now I wasn't at all sure of their purpose. I jammed the accelerator to the floorboards. Traffic was fairly sparse but still dangerous. Cars got in my way and I had to slow down now and then.

I was needling toward ninety and they were gaining, about a quarter mile back, when we approached the Sunset intersection. I saw the patrol car make the turn from it to the highway just ahead and was caught in a panic of indecision. There were bad cops and there were good cops. They were all looking for me.

I went past the patrol car doing ninety. It must have taken the driver no more than two beats, while his mouth fell open. The red light flared and they rocketed after me with full siren, Santella and Yeager slowing to trail in their wake.

For a while I pulled away. But the rental had been abused and was begging for mercy at ninety-six. The red eye winked malevolently closer and the siren grew upon my ears. At that speed they don't write tickets. They consider you a drunk or a maniac who should be behind bars until the judge frowns down upon you in the morning. And in my wallet, my license read Glenn Harley. Much worse than no license at all.

I searched frantically for some brilliant maneuver and there wasn't any. Then I swayed past a truck and into the first decent curve. The red eye closed from view.

104

I had a few seconds' grace and when I saw the motel with the vacancy sign, I prayed hard and braked harder. I nearly turned over but it was a big driveway and I slid into it with the rear-end skidding, cut my lights and faded around the back of the building into a parking space as I heard them go by.

I went over to the little office and paid for a room. I was at the window with the lights out when I saw both cars flash by, retracing. I got undressed and went to bed.

But not to sleep.

19...

The following day I checked out and drove back to the Palisades Hotel. En route I stopped at a hardware store and bought a roll-tape measure, a hammer and small nails. After fixing one of the beds so that it appeared slept in, I had breakfast in the suite and read the morning paper. The story was still on the front page. A wide search for me was "closing in." Lieutenant Howard Purcell of the Homicide Squad hinted "mysteriously" that round-the-clock police efforts had uncovered a new angle and that my arrest was "imminent." I had no doubt that this mysterious new angle was my phone call of the day before.

Meanwhile, the story continued, funeral arrangements for Norman Rainey were in progress. Services and interment would be at Forest Lawn. A turnout of unprecedented proportions was expected, including some of the biggest stars of the movie kingdom.

During the morning, after the maid had cleaned the disorder I had faked, I again checked the layout of the suite. There was a small sitting room, a bedroom and bath in 710. I decided to use this as the meeting place. There was a connecting door from the sitting room into the bedroom and bath of 709. With the roll-tape I measured the height of the door and the length of the wall in which it was set. I wrote down the figures. I made a study of the room's decor. I went out.

When I came back some time later I unwrapped a heavy white drape with a simple design in color harmony with the room. It took me two hours to complete what would pass for a professional job, but I had covered the entire wall from the floor to a height just above the door frame. Ruffles and folds hid the nails.

I moved the desk and sofa against this wall in such a manner that they did not block the door. Then I stood back and surveyed my handiwork. It was better than I had hoped. The drape gave the room a touch of added splendor. I could imagine the look on the maid's face when she came in the following day, and the astonished reaction of some assistant manager.

At six o'clock I phoned Grinstead.

"Have the Rhymer girl in the lobby of the Palisades Hotel, near the desk, at eight o'clock," I said. "And be on time. Harley will phone at eight-fifteen sharp and he won't make the call twice. And, Grinstead—no more clever tricks like last night, or we don't play."

I hung up.

I went down to the lobby and got the briefcase from the safe. I told the clerk my business friends had been delayed and I would continue to hold the rooms. I took the case to 522, where I hid it with the hammer, my wallet and all other identification. I went up to the suite and concealed the .45 and the keys to the other rooms behind the section of drape in back of the desk. And on the desk was the phone.

Now I was ready.

The hotel had a mezzanine with writing desks, chairs and sofas. It was a railed balcony overlooking the lobby. I sat in a chair behind the rail and peeked down through the wrought-iron supports. I could see the reservation desk plainly.

I was there a half hour early. Waiting, I got the worst

107

case of nerves since the whole nightmare began. I kept going over and over the plan, seeing a dozen possibilities for error. I started to wonder if Grinstead with his poker face had guessed my identity. And, above all, I wondered if I would be looking down at Nancy Rhymer or some substitute with whom they hoped to fool Ralph Barnett. Yet the way I had set up the deal, how could they fool Glenn Harley on the phone? It went round and round, while I lighted one cigarette from another, while I kept drying the sweaty palms of my hands on a handkerchief.

Then, at five minutes to eight, I saw Grinstead come into the hotel. Alone. He stood close to the desk, scanning the lobby foot by foot. He said something to the clerk, who moved out of sight, returned and shook his head.

Grinstead frowned, searched the lobby again and strode out the door.

I didn't know what to do. My plan called for abandoning the idea if they didn't show with Nancy. I sat fidgeting, trying to decide. And while I pondered, Grinstead came back into the lobby. Behind him were Santella and Yeager.

And walking between them was Nancy Rhymer.

She wore the same turquoise wool-knit suit in which I had seen her last. And she managed to look just as beautiful in it, though her face was straining with tension. The sight of her gave me a moment of relief, disturbing the old longings. The feeling passed in an instant and I hated the bitch.

I went to a booth in the lobby, dialed Lieutenant Purcell at Homicide. He wasn't in but had left a number where he could be reached. I called it. After identifying myself as Carl Quinn, I said, "Stand by to pick up Harley with Rainey's killer, Lieutenant. I'll ring back within the hour and give you the location."

From the suite I called down and had Grinstead summoned to the house phone. "Bring the girl up to 710," I told him.

Meanwhile I gave my disguise a nervous check in the mirror and set up the room so there was enough light—but not too much. Then I sat at the desk by the phone and waited. In a couple of minutes there was a knock at the door. I looked at my watch. It was six minutes after eight.

"It's open," I called in my Ralph Barnett tenor.

Grinstead came in first, followed by Nancy, then Santella and Yeager. Santella closed the door and locked it. I remained seated.

My eyes touched Nancy's. Her face was expressionless. Grinstead waved her to a chair next to the desk and she sat down. Santella, his mouth as ever busy with a wad of gum, gave me a cool glance before he began to rove around the room, turning over cushions, looking underneath everything, opening a table drawer, leaning out the window, his head turning right and left. He came back, paused in front of the drape, eying it curiously.

I froze in my chair. No one spoke.

Santella reached out and touched the material, fingering it. He turned suddenly to Yeager. "C'mon," he said. "We'll have a look in there."

They strode into the bedroom and I began to breathe again.

I reached in my pocket and got out a picture of Nancy which I used to carry in my wallet. I looked at the picture and then at her, pointedly.

"Where did you get the photo?" said Grinstead, reaching down to yank the desk drawer open to inspect inside it.

"Harley mailed it to me," I answered, listening to Santella and Yeager rattling around in the other room.

Nancy looked at me sharply but it was impossible to tell what she was thinking. Santella and Yeager came back into the room. Santella said, "Checks out okay. Just a bedroom and bath. No bags, no clothes, nothin'."

109

Grinstead nodded, closed the drawer.

I laid the snapshot on the desk. "I'm satisfied this is Nancy Rhymer," I said. "Let's see the confession."

"Stand up!" said Yeager.

"Are you talking to me, sonny?" I said.

"You heard him!" Santella snapped.

"And who are you?"

"I'm a big fist in your face if you don't stand up."

I looked at Grinstead. And at my watch. "If my voice doesn't come over that phone in five minutes, you've lost out. He won't talk to anyone else."

"We just want to see if you're carrying a weapon," explained Grinstead.

I shrugged and stood.

Santella ran his hands over my body in the police manner, saying, "This guy's got muscles for his age." My heart did a flip. But no one seemed interested. "Now turn your pockets inside out."

I gave him a look, sighed, obeyed. I put car keys, the key to 710, forty-six dollars and change, a ballpoint, on the desk.

"That all you got, wise guy?" said Yeager, picking up the key to 710. "Where's your wallet?"

Again I looked at my watch. "Three minutes," I said. "And I haven't seen the confession." I put the stuff back in my pockets. Yeager held the key to 710 in his hand.

Grinstead nodded. "All right, Nancy," he said.

Nancy opened her purse and produced a piece of folded paper, handed it to me, dead pan. She hadn't said a word since she entered the room.

I unfolded the paper and studied it. The confession was identical with the one I had typed. It was in the handwriting I remembered from her address book. It was unsigned.

"Sit here at the desk, Miss Rhymer," I said, getting out my pen.

110

She came over and sat down, taking the pen. A familiar fragrance clung to her. "I want you to add one line and sign it," I said.

"What line?" said Grinstead. "You didn't . . ."

I held up my hand. "Just write this: 'I swear that I am of sound mind and body and that I make the above statement without duress.'"

I leaned over her shoulder and she wrote as I had dictated, then signed. And that was precisely when I was sure that I had been right. It was a farce. Nancy would never have signed that paper unless she expected to leave with it in company of Grinstead and his boys, taking a promised share of three hundred forty-five thousand for herself.

I handed her the confession and told her to keep it until I called for it. She put it back in her purse, returned to her chair as I sank behind the desk. For the first time she spoke, leaning tensely forward.

"Marvin," she said. "Haven't you got any heart? Won't you give me a break? You read today's paper. They'll catch him and you'll get your money. Please, Marvin. Please! Don't be cruel. Why do you have to sacrifice me and—"

"Shut up!" barked Grinstead.

"Marvin, I beg you. I beg you not to!"

"I don't give a goddam what happens to you as long as I get my dough," said Grinstead. "So knock it off!"

Her face folded and she broke into tears. It was her best performance on or off stage. I was unmoved.

"How long will it take this messenger to get here?" asked Grinstead.

"Harley says not over ten minutes, if he's satisfied."

I looked at my watch and it was fifteen after. My God, had they forgotten? Why didn't that call come!

The four of them had turned to look at me in grim silence, Nancy with dried eyes and the first shadow of suspicion on her face. Yeager shifted in position, Santella

111

stared at his watch. Next to me I could hear Grinstead breathing heavily, his eyes on the phone. A little thing like the sound of that bell. And yet unless it rang. . . .

And then it did!

They all jerked nervously, and bent forward. I picked up the receiver and held it so tight against my ear it was painful.

"Hello," I said.

"Mr. Quinn?" The mechanical voice of the operator.

"Yeah, speaking."

"This is the operator. You left a call, sir. It's eight-fifteen."

"She's here, all right," I said. "The paper checks and she signed it. Hold on and I'll clear the room; then you can talk to her."

The operator was patiently explaining that I had misunderstood, but I put the phone in my lap and held my hand over the earpiece. Grinstead was crowding me. He held out his hand.

"Gimme that!" he said. "Lemme talk to the sonofabitch first."

"Out!" I said. "Everyone but Miss Rhymer out—or I hang up."

I saw that Santella was taking a .38 from his holster, and Yeager was moving in. The plan was falling apart. I started to hang up. But then Grinstead waved Santella off, said, "All right, all right! One minute. No more." On the way out, Yeager tried the key in the door, then closed it.

And we were alone.

I stood with the phone. As I held the receiver toward Nancy, I disconnected with my thumb.

"He just wants to ask you a couple of questions, Miss Rhymer," I said. "I'm going to listen with you." I knelt down beside her chair. And the moment she took the receiver, I reached in back of the curtain and found the .45.

She never quite got the third hello out of her mouth. It was cut short when I brought the gun down on her head—a quick, stunning blow but not a dangerous one. She gave a little moan and collapsed in her chair. I grabbed the phone as it was falling from her hand.

I got the keys from behind the drape, opened the door to 709 quietly, then picked up Nancy and carried her through. I laid her on the bed, tiptoed back for her purse, then locked the connecting door. My sweep-hand said twenty-five seconds had passed.

Now I unlocked the door to 709 and cautiously peeked out. The little hallway was empty. Around the corner I heard Grinstead say, "I don't hear a goddam thing."

"Let's break it up." That was Santella.

"In fifteen seconds," said Grinstead.

I opened the door wide and dashed back. I cradled Nancy in my arms. Her head lolled. I tucked it against my shoulder and went out into the hall with her, pulling the door almost to with my foot, then closing it gently with a hand underneath Nancy.

I carried her around the bend to the main corridor just as someone was stepping onto an elevator. He didn't see us and I literally ran with her to the stairs. She was getting heavy and I was glad we were going down.

On the fifth floor it looked as if the gods were with me. No one was about. And then, just as I was fifteen feet from 522, the door to 524 opened and a young couple stepped into the coridor. Either I had to go right on past them or reverse course. I walked on.

I almost bumped into them.

"God," said the young man. "What's wrong? You need some help, buddy?"

"No thanks," I said heartily. "The wife just had one too many. Gonna put 'er to beddy-bye." I kept moving.

"Poor thing," said the woman behind me. I knew they were staring.

113

I sat Nancy against the wall while I opened the door. When I picked her up, she stirred in my arms. I carried her in and closed the door with my foot, catching a last glimpse of the couple, still staring open-mouthed.

I laid her on the bed and locked the door. I got the confession from her purse and put it in my pocket. I bathed her face with cold water, ran my hand over her head. There was a small egg in the welter of hair. I couldn't see any blood. I was bending over her when her eyes slowly opened.

"Well, Nancy," I said in my own voice. "Everyone has his day. And this is mine."

20...

Her eyes widened. She sat up abruptly, winced, held her head and fell back.

"What happened?" she groaned. "I was talking to—"

"Glenn Harley?"

"Yes. No, he didn't come on and then . . . Oh, I don't know."

"I had to hit you over the head, Nancy. It was almost a pleasure. And then I carried you into the next room and down here."

I walked to the window, parted the drape. Below was the swimming pool, and to the left the main entrance to the hotel. I saw no one. When I turned, Nancy was sitting up, staring vacantly around the room.

Her eyes fastened on me, sharpened. Her expression was oddly intense. "What room is this?" she asked.

"522," I answered. "Two floors below."

"It doesn't matter," she said. "I just wanted to hear your voice again."

She leaped off the bed and hurled herself at the door. She had it partway open when I got to her and slammed it shut again. She fought me all the way back to the bed. I shoved her down and held her.

"Don't try that again," I said. "You could get mauled."

Looking up at me, her eyes were vicious. "I know

115

you," she said. "I know you, Glenn. I was coming close when we were still upstairs. Another few minutes . . . But the voice fooled me. Oh God, oh God, how I hate you!"

I walked away, sat down with my hand on the phone. "You hate *me*," I said. "That's a laugh." From my change pocket I fished a little scrap of paper which Grinstead and company had missed. On it was written Lieutenant Purcell's number.

Nancy's long fingers examined her head gingerly. "They'll find us," she said. "They'll be here any minute now."

I shook my head. "No they won't, Nancy. There are over seven hundred rooms in this hotel. And I'm registered as Quinn, not Barnett. Besides, I doubt if it would ever occur to them that we're in another room. They would just naturally assume that I forced you right out of the hotel and into my car. That's why it's so neat, Nancy."

"Why did you do it?" she hissed. "Why did you tell where the body was? Because you found the money!" she shouted. "Isn't that it? And you wanted the police off your neck. So you told. You turned me in."

"Why, Nancy," I said, "I didn't turn you in. But I'm going to. Right now."

I picked up the phone, lifted the receiver.

"Liar!" she screamed. "While I was with Mary Ann, you were giving the whole story to the police, selling me out, selling your soul for money!"

"Order, please," said the operator.

I looked at Nancy. On her face was real hatred. She wasn't acting.

"Your order, please," said the operator.

"Never mind." I cradled the receiver.

"Nancy," I said, "you've done everything but personally escort me to the gas chamber. You've made me Public Enemy Number One—with every trigger-happy cop in the state on the prowl for me. At best I may get a year, and when I come out no one would hire me as a prop boy. And yet you try to tell me that I sold *you* out to the police. That's so goddam funny I'm going to gamble two minutes to listen to it. Sing it nice and pretty, Nancy. Let's hear it."

"If I had a gun," she said quietly, "I'd kill you. Because they can only execute me once."

"You're better with knives," I said. "Come on. Let's hear how I sold you out. I'd like to know how I did it."

She sat very still on the edge of the bed and a subtle change came to her face, a kind of groping.

"Well," she said, "didn't you? Marvin said you did."

"He said I did what?"

"That while I was with Mary Ann, Santella and Yeager went to your apartment and questioned you. They accused you of killing Norman Rainey and stealing the money. And the minute they mentioned the money, you told them I did it and exactly where the body was hidden."

I began to see that she might be telling the truth. I said, "And you believed a guy like Grinstead?"

"Of course. Because if you didn't tell the police where to find the body, who did? After all, there wasn't another person in the world besides you and me who knew where it was hidden. What else could I think?"

"You didn't think hard enough. Why would I tell? What would I have to gain? Did you ask Grinstead that one?"

"Sure I asked him what you had to gain. And you know what he said?"

"I can't imagine. Unless it had something to do with money."

"Right. He said you admitted to Santella and Yeager that things had been going badly for you and you were broke. You needed money. You were keeping quiet, covering for me in the hope of finding it for yourself. Then

117

when you didn't find the money, you had no interest in risking jail by protecting me any longer. Especially since the police promised you immunity if you told the truth. You were quoted as saying you weren't going to be a sucker for some cheap little whore when there was nothing in it for you but trouble. That's what you told the police."

"You call them police? Santella and Yeager?"

"That's what they are, good or bad. And, as Marvin said, you didn't know the difference."

"So they told you all these lies and then what?"

"Well, I was terribly scared. Because they said you would talk and it would all come out sooner or later. They offered to help if I would tell them what I did with the money. I was so angry and frightened I said you found it and hid it. I figured that was still possible and anyway, I would get them off my neck. They told me not to worry about you, they'd take care of it. Just leave it to them. Meantime, they said it was best for me to hide out at Marvin's beach house in Malibu. Glenn, don't lie to me now, when it doesn't matter. You did tell them where to find the body, didn't you?"

"No. You fell for an old police trick. We both did. They played one of us against the other."

"My God!" she moaned. "Then what really *did* happen?"

Pacing about the room, I told her.

"And the money?" she asked. "Where is it now?"

"It's hidden right here. I was about to turn it over to the police."

Her face softened. Suddenly she ran across the room and threw her arms around me. "Glenn," she said, "oh, Glenn. Once I loved you and then I hated you. And now I could love you again."

I kissed her. The bitterness went out of me and I felt myself returning to her. Yet where did that leave us but in a deeper complication?

118

We sat down beside each other on the bed. I put my arm around her. We were both silent in our private thoughts, adjusting.

"I've got it!" she said.

"Got what?"

"I think I know how Marvin caught on to me."

"That you killed Rainey? How?"

"He came out to the beach house yesterday and found me drinking. In fact, I . . . I was nearly drunk. I got started and I couldn't stop. I was so nervous all the time. And he said to me, 'You know, Nancy, you've got to cut out the booze. You never used to drink anything but wine. It's a dead giveaway. Any dope who knew you would guess that you were cracking up with the strain.' And that's how he must have figured it out."

"Still don't get it," I said.

"Well, the day he came over to my house while you were there, remember, I was gulping down straight bourbon right in front of him. It was the one thing I forgot. He knew I must be positively shaking inside, and he put two and two together."

"You mean he put one and one together," I said. "You and I. And then he called Santella and Yeager and while you were gone maybe they went over the grounds and found something suspicious. It wouldn't take much. A button from a shirt near that cliff. Or a cigarette butt. Or the mark of a rope."

"Or footprints in the dirt where you slid down," she said.

"God! I never thought to cover up. We were real amateurs."

"They kept me away," she said. "And then the minute it got dark they must have come over and started digging and . . . Oh, it doesn't matter any more. But, Glenn, what shall we do now? That's all that's important."

I took her hand and squeezed. "It's over, Nancy. Why

don't you face it? Finally. We'll have a talk with Lieutenant Purcell, who's in charge of the case. I'll turn the money over to him and we'll tell him the whole story about Rainey. About Santella and Yeager. About Grinstead and his filthy parties with the blackmail payoff."

"How did you know!" she gasped.

"Mary Ann DeGraw told me. But let me finish. We'll get a good attorney. Somehow I'll borrow the money. We'll expose the whole dirty mess. Sympathy will be on your side. You acted in self-defense. Don't you see?"

She took her hand from mine, gave me a little pat on the shoulder. "Poor Glenn," she said, and stood. Her face had drained of color. With a trance-like expression, she began to walk aimlessly about the room, wringing her hands. "A hundred and seventy million people," she whimpered. "Reading the slimy dregs of my life. The pictures, and the dirty, smelly jail . . ."

She broke off. "You have the confession?" she asked in a distant voice.

"In my pocket."

"Good. That will help, won't it?" She spoke to herself, nodding her head and washing her hands. "It's so terribly stuffy, I can't think. Could we have some air?"

I saw that she really was physically sick. She seemed to be wilting, ready to faint. I got up and opened the window.

"Why don't you lie down for a minute," I said. "We needn't hurry."

She shook her head firmly. "No! No, I'm all right."

She crossed to the window, parted the curtain slightly and drew in a deep breath.

"I could have loved you, Glenn," she said. "If things had been different."

There was an odd little smile on her face. It set me on edge. Her hand clenched so tight around the curtain that the knuckles bleached. And at that instant I knew.

When she hurled the curtain aside and dove, I was

already up and running. I grabbed her leg but it slithered through my fingers as she went out. Then her foot caught in my hands and I held with all my might. Five stories above a cement walk, she dangled head down into the night. And struggled to break free.

Her shoe had fallen off and I felt her stockinged foot slip slowly through my sweaty fingers. She was crawling down the wall, pulling, kicking, out of my grasp. In seconds she would be gone.

I had to take the chance. Quickly I let one hand go and grabbed the other foot. I heaved back and pulled her sobbing into the room.

She sagged against me. I clutched her, supporting her weight.

"Why . . . why didn't you let me go?" she gulped. "You . . . you can't stop me. . . . You can't, you can't! Sooner or later," she sobbed, "sooner or later, I'll do it. . . ."

I half carried her to a chair and stood over her.

"Oh God," I said. "You mean it, don't you?"

She nodded. Her head drooped. I lifted her chin, looked into the moist beauty of her eyes.

"All right," I said, "then we won't do it. We'll find another way. There's three hundred fifty thousand here. And I love you. So stop crying, baby, stop crying." I sucked in a long breath.

"In an hour," I said, "we'll be on our way to the other side of the world."

I took her confession out of my pocket and began to tear it to shreds.

21...

There was a plane leaving for Hawaii at midnight. It wasn't exactly the other side of the world, but it was some two thousand miles of ocean away. It was a jumping-off place for the Orient and you didn't need a passport. A reservation clerk told me they would hold two tickets for us at the airport.

"Well," I said, when I hung up, "I'm just as glad we won't leave here until eleven. The Grinstead crew may still be lurking around. But by eleven they should be hunting elsewhere."

"Won't the police be watching the airport?" said Nancy. Her eyes were bright and dry; her spirit had returned.

"They could be," I said. "And I don't mean Santella and Yeager, either. But aren't you forgetting something?"

"What?"

"Have you looked at me lately?"

She stared, then began to laugh. "I see what you mean. You don't look at all like Glenn Harley. Really, you're just too ancient to be traveling with me."

"That's no way to talk to your lovable old husband, Mrs. Quinn."

"I don't know about lovable," she came back. "But

you're old. And wealthy." She looked down at the briefcase which I had just opened for her wide-eyed inspection. Her face grew serious.

"They won't be searching for me at all, will they?
The legitimate police."

"No. Why should they be?"

"Glenn, darling. I feel so guilty. They should be hunting for *me*. It's such a dirty trick on you."

"Yes, but if you're going to be jumping out windows . . . Let's change the subject for now, huh?" I
looked at my watch. "Five after nine. By this time
Lieutenant Purcell will be swearing I was just another fake getting my kicks on the phone. Well, we've
got two hours. What do we do now?"

She fell back on the bed and the smile spread slowly
across her face.

"Darling," she said, "Don't be naive."

I got up from my chair and walked toward her.

It was twenty minutes to eleven and she was asleep
beside me, one leg draped over mine, an arm around my
waist. She had a rare talent for sleeping in a crisis. I had
not been able to shut my eyes. And now the sweet inter-
mission was over and a still more breathless tension was
in me. It was nearly finished, and yet I was immeasurably
depressed. I reached across her and turned on the lamp.

I took one look at the firm rich contours of that
exquisite body, kissed a bare shoulder and shook her
gently awake. As she would for a long time to come, she
came alive with a start, sitting up and looking at me as
the stranger I was.

"For a minute I didn't know you," she said without
humor. "What time is it?"

"Time to get moving," I said.

We got dressed quickly and silently. I decided to
leave everything but the briefcase and the gun. Clothes
could be bought in Hawaii.

Ready first, I stood by nervously as she applied make-up. She had taken a comb from her purse and was fixing her hair with it when the phone rang.

We looked at each other. The bell sound stopped, pulsed again, jangling inside me.

"What is it?" she cried hysterically. "Did you ask them to wake you?"

I gave my head a negative shake and stared at the phone.

"Answer it!" she said.

"No! They must be checking. It can only mean trouble. C'mon. Let's get out of here!"

I grabbed the briefcase and put the .45 in my hip pocket. I opened the door cautiously. The corridor was empty. We ran to the stairs and raced down to the main floor. I opened the door and looked. A few people milled about the lobby, all of them strangers.

"Two exits," I said. "We'll take the back one, slow and easy."

We walked casually across the lobby, turned left past a newsstand and a barber shop, and came to the exit. I motioned for Nancy to stand out of sight, placed myself at the corner of the glass door and cautiously looked out.

Just beyond the door, at the left, stood Grinstead, watching. Across from him, spread-legged, a cigarette dangling from his mouth, was Yeager.

I took Nancy's hand and led her away, explaining as we clipped along. "Our only chance is the front, then," I said. "They might not believe we'd risk anything so bold."

We went down a flight of steps, approached the main entrance and stepped out of view. Again I looked. A uniformed policeman stood just outside talking to a man in plain clothes.

"God almighty," I said. "Two more. Strangers. One in uniform. Is it an accident or did they send for help?"

"What do we do now?" said Nancy, furiously biting her lip.

I tried to think, came up with jumbled fragments of ideas leading nowhere. Then I remembered the bar.

We moved toward it as if in some frantic dream, rushing in a hopeless maze of sealed doors.

The darkness of the bar gave some small relief. Couples murmured intimately across their tables. Voices at the bar were gay and strident, rising above the swell of a Hammond organ. Another world from ours—oblivious.

At the back of the room there was another glass door, opening upon the pool. We ignored the hovering waitress and moved toward it, then ducked back.

"I don't see anyone," said Nancy.

"We don't have a choice," I said.

We went out. No one waited to stop us.

We skirted the pool, then crossed a lawn heavy with shrubs and palms to the parking lot, a dim unattended area close by the street.

"Made it!" said Nancy as I found the Olds and unlocked the door.

That was when Anthony Santella stepped out of the shadows behind a gun. "Going somewhere?" he said.

I watched his jaw work lazily and thought, well, this is the end of it, anyway. Unless . . .

"Sure," I said. "I was going somewhere. But I just changed my mind."

I had turned toward him and Nancy was just behind me. As I spoke, I took her hand and guided it toward my hip pocket, then raised my own hands for Santella to see, awkwardly, because I had the case under my arm.

"You can go and join your boyfriend now, Nancy," I said. "You belong to each other."

I felt the sudden loss of weight as Nancy removed the gun from my pocket.

"Yeah, Nancy," said Santella. "And when you come,

125

you bring that briefcase over to me, like a good girl."

She slid the briefcase from under my arm and walked toward him, holding the .45 in back of it. When she was close to him she stepped to one side, the gun flew up and swooped down over his head. But he saw it coming, ducked and caught the blow on his shoulder. He staggered, recovered.

By that time I was on top of him. He fired blindly as I walloped him on the side of the head with a left and delivered a right so powerful that his mouth became a crimson mash. He swayed back, brought the gun up swiftly. I was looking right into the barrel. But Nancy was behind him and when she struck him with the .45 this time, he was out before he hit the ground.

I picked up the case and we ran for the car. I got the wrong key in the switch and Nancy kept saying, "Hurry, hurry! They must have heard that shot."

Then the motor caught and we roared toward the exit. I saw two men running from the hotel, but couldn't make them out. We swayed onto the street, flashed over to Wilshire and sped east.

At Sepulveda we turned again and still there was no sign of a tail in my rearview mirror. I looked at my watch, said, "We've still got time, Nancy. We'll make it!"

She didn't answer. She hadn't spoken a word since we left the lot. We flew on, swerving dangerously around slow traffic.

At the airport intersection there was a patrol car waiting off the road. I held my breath, but they were traffic control and didn't even notice us. Nancy still sat silent and morose in her corner.

But as I yanked her into the terminal building, racing her toward the ticket counter, she suddenly pulled away, stopped dead.

"In God's name, what's the matter with you?" I snapped.

126

She gave me one searching look and tears came to her eyes.

"Why do we hurry?" she said. "We'll be hurrying all our lives. There'll always be shadows, everywhere we go in the whole world. And I'm already so terribly tired."

"What in hell are you talking about, Nancy? We'll miss that plane!"

"We're not going, Glenn. It's not fair to you. It never was. And pretty soon you'd hate me for the awful coward I am, letting you be chased around the earth for a crime I committed—making a thief out of you, besides."

"And when did you come to that decision?" I asked.

"It started when we were in the bar," she said. "And I saw all those people having a good time with no more problems than a hangover in the morning. And I knew that everywhere we would find people just like them, having the same commonplace fun. And we might even be with them, but we'd never be part of them. We'd always be the outsiders."

"It's true," I said. "And I've known it all along. But are you sure? I mean, you wouldn't . . ."

"Jump out a window again? No, I'm over that." She smiled wryly. "And the windows in jails have bars, don't they?"

I kissed her and she took my hand and led me out of the terminal. We got back in the car and began to drive, very slowly. When we got to the intersection, she said, "There's that same police car over there."

"I know."

"I want to stop and do it now. Before I change my mind. All right?"

"It's almost funny," I said. "There's nothing for *you* to do. Don't you remember? They're looking for *me*."

I peeled off the wig and the mustache, put the glasses in my pocket, and plucked the briefcase from the seat. We got out and crossed the highway to the police car.

127

The policemen looked very average and not unfriendly.

"Help you people?" said the one on the passenger side, with his cap pushed back on his head.

"Yes," I said. "I suppose you might call it that. My name is Glenn Harley. . . ."

THE END

of an Original Gold Medal Novel by

Robert Colby